Additional Praise for
The Wife of Martin Guerre

"One of the most significant short novels in English."
—*Atlantic Monthly*

"When the literary history of the second millennium is written at the end of the third, in the category of dazzling American short fiction [Janet Lewis's] *Wife of Martin Guerre* will be regarded as the 20th century's *Billy Budd* and Janet Lewis will be ranked with Herman Melville." —*New York Times*

"Flaubertian in the elegance of its form and the gravity of its style."
—*New Yorker*

"Janet Lewis brings the haunting qualities of fable to this novella, based on a legal case that attracted wide attention in 16th-century France and has continued to fascinate down through the years."
—Ron Hansen, *Wall Street Journal*

"I found myself weeping. The calm detail, the observation of things that continue in nature despite our own vicissitudes, the underspoken humanity of the writing: it was a combination of these, and something magically beautiful in the choice of words besides—for Janet Lewis was a fine poet as well as novelist."
—Vikram Seth, *Sunday Telegraph* (London)

"*The Wife of Martin Guerre* by Janet Lewis is one of the most resonant short novels I can remember."
—Evan S. Connell, Jr., *Bookforum*

"One of the best short novels in English."
—Bruce Allen, *Christian Science Monitor*

"Reading the three novels in a line, from *The Wife of Martin Guerre* to *The Ghost of Monsieur Scarron*, is a powerful experience. . . . In each there is a fully and vividly realized woman who finds herself twisting helplessly in the dilemmas posed by love and duty."
—Larry McMurtry, *New York Review of Books*

The Wife of Martin Guerre

Swallow Press books by Janet Lewis

The Wife of Martin Guerre
The Trial of Sören Qvist
The Ghost of Monsieur Scarron
Good-Bye, Son and Other Stories
Poems Old and New, 1918–1978
Selected Poems of Janet Lewis

The Wife of
Martin Guerre

JANET LEWIS

Introduction by Kevin Haworth
Afterword by Larry McMurtry

SWALLOW PRESS — OHIO UNIVERSITY PRESS
ATHENS, OHIO

Swallow Press
An imprint of Ohio University Press, Athens, Ohio 45701
www.ohioswallow.com

Printed in the United States of America
Swallow Press/Ohio University Press books are
printed on acid-free paper ⊗ ™

23 22 21 20 19 18 17 13   5 4 3 2 1

Library of Congress Cataloging-in-Publication Data

Lewis, Janet, 1899–1998.
The wife of Martin Guerre / Janet Lewis ; introduction by Kevin
Haworth ; afterword by Larry McMurtry.
   pages ; cm.
Includes bibliographical references.
ISBN 978-0-8040-1143-3 (pb : acid-free paper) — ISBN 978-0-8040-4053-2
(electronic)
1. Guerre, Bertrande de Rols, active 1539–1560 — Fiction. 2. Guerre,
Martin, active 1539–1560 — Fiction. 3. Impostors and imposture — Fiction.
4. France — Fiction. I. Title.
PS3523.E866W55 2013
813'.52 — dc23
                        2013016158

Contents

Introduction

The Wife of Martin Guerre, Janet Lewis's most celebrated novel, emerged from the gift of a good book from husband to wife. Sometime in the 1930s the renowned poet Yvor Winters gave his wife and fellow writer Lewis an old law book, Samuel March Phillips's *Famous Cases of Circumstantial Evidence*, thinking that she might find it helpful after she mentioned that she was having trouble with one of her plots.

From that thoughtful writerly gift grew the three novels of *Cases of Circumstantial Evidence*, of which *The Wife of Martin Guerre* is by far the most famous. Already the author of one historical novel, *The Invasion*, Lewis was drawn to the story of Bertrande de Rols, married at age eleven to the young son of a powerful landowner. "One morning in January, 1539," Lewis writes, "a wedding was celebrated in the village of Artigues." From that simple opening line Lewis spins a short novel of astonishing depth and resonance, a sharply drawn historical tale that asks contemporary questions about identity and belonging, about men and women, and about an individual's capacity to act within an inflexible system.

Lewis's plot closely follows the string of events cited in Phillips's 1874 legal history. Because of a dispute with his father, ambitious Martin Guerre leaves his wife Bertrande and their young son, intending to return when he can fully claim his inheritance. He finally returns, eight years later, to a woman who has grown in maturity and in her sense of belonging to the world around her. Or does he? The man who comes walking down the road *looks like* Martin Guerre, knows things that Martin Guerre would know. But there is something in the way he speaks to his wife, a note of kindness, in fact, that makes Bertrande wonder. Is it Martin Guerre after all?

From this question grows that most unusual of literary forms—a short novel that does its work so efficiently that it feels as substantial as a novel many pages longer. It is no surprise, then, that *The Wife of Martin Guerre* has drawn comparisons with the greatest short novels in American literature. "The 20th century's *Billy Budd*," the *New York Times* calls it.[1] Larry McMurtry, no stranger to novels both short and long, writes in the *New York Review of Books* that *Martin Guerre* is a "masterpiece. . . . a short novel that can run with *Billy Budd, The Spoils of Poynton, Seize the Day,* or any other."[2] Every few years another writer or critic will weigh in, urging readers to "rediscover" Lewis as she has been rediscovered so many times before.

So what is it that gives *The Wife of Martin Guerre* such continuing interest? Much of it is rooted in Lewis's portrait of Bertrande, a woman who grows steadily in confidence as the novel progresses, and who possesses a fierce moral sense that guides her actions even at great personal cost. Lewis's portrayal of the legal system, while fascinating in its own right, also acts to amplify the moral issues at play. The law operates around questions of evidence, oftentimes incomplete or circumstantial, which nonetheless must be resolved by absolute conclusions of guilt or innocence. At the same time, the law often fails to address what is *right*, or what a woman like Bertrande knows in her heart to be true.

The strength of this conundrum has given *The Wife of Martin Guerre* a long life, extended by two popular film adaptations. The first film, a 1982 French version titled *Le Retour de Martin Guerre*, recognizes Lewis's contribution to the story by giving her author's credit. The second, a 1993 version titled *Sommersby*, resets the action to the American South during the upheaval of the Reconstruction period following the Civil War. Both films devote extended screen time to their famous male leads—Gerard Depardieu in the French version, Richard Gere in the American one—thus creating a story that is as much about the husband as it is about the wife. But Lewis felt that both the specific setting of *The Wife of Martin Guerre* and the focus on Bertrande's decision making are critical parts of the novel's essence. The strict Catholic morality of sixteenth-century France serves both as a guiding force for Bertrande and as a prison; once she believes she has committed adultery, as Lewis notes, "her way was laid out for her."[3] At the same time, *The Wife of Martin Guerre* is much more than a simple morality play. Bertrande struggles on many levels—against the limited roles afforded to her as a woman, against her husband in both subtle and forceful ways, and finally with her own knowledge of the man standing in front of her.

This close attention to an individual's moral choices in the face of strange circumstance links *The Wife of Martin Guerre* with the two novels that follow in the *Cases of Circumstantial Evidence* series. Though each of the novels stands on its own, they remain united by their shared origins in the history of law, discovered by Lewis in the same legal casebook where she first found the story of Bertrande de Rols and Martin Guerre. The setting shifts to seventeenth-century Denmark in *The Trial of Sören Qvist*, which focuses on a devoted parson, albeit one with a harsh temper, who is accused of killing one of his workers. Again the law closes in on a man who may or may not be guilty, and again the characters struggle as much with their own consciences and the changing times as they do with the ambiguous legal facts in front of them. In *The Ghost of Monsieur Scarron*, Lewis returns to France, this time during the reign of Louis XIV. In this longest and in some ways most complex of the three novels, a bookbinder becomes enmeshed in a political drama that spirals out of control—the king is denounced in a pamphlet, leading to criminal charges—but the real crime is domestic, an adulterous affair that contributes to the tragedy as much as the public trial that follows.

In each case Lewis focuses her rigorous but sympathetic eye on those trapped by the circumstances, particularly the women burdened by a system that gives most of its power to men. In his retrospective on Lewis's career that appeared in the *New York Review of Books*, written the year of Lewis's death, Larry McMurtry declares, "Reading the three novels in a line, from *The Wife of Martin Guerre* to *The Ghost of Monsieur Scarron*, is a powerful experience. Though all three were based on actual cases in the law, their power is literary not legal. . . . In each the ruin of an honest person is complete, and in each there is a fully and vividly realized woman who finds herself twisting helplessly in the dilemmas posed by love and duty."[4]

Years after the initial publication of *The Wife of Martin Guerre*, Lewis continued to investigate the tragedy of Bertrande, consulting additional sources as they found their way to her. Likewise the novel itself traveled through several publishers and editions before finding a permanent home with Alan Swallow, founder of Swallow Press and longtime champion of Lewis's husband Winters and other contemporary writers. Swallow claimed that in all his years selling *The Wife of Martin Guerre* and recommending it to friends, he "never found one who didn't admire the work."[5] As for the truth behind the lives of Bertrande and Martin, Lewis herself notes simply, "In the end, many questions remain unanswered."[6] It is no wonder that novels of such enduring mystery could come from a woman with a long and fascinating life of her own.

The Life and Legacy of Janet Lewis

Janet Lewis was born in Chicago in 1898 and attended high school in Oak Park, where she and schoolmate Ernest Hemingway both contributed to the school literary magazine. Like Hemingway, she spent many youthful summers "up in

Michigan," a place that figures prominently in her short stories, much as it does in his. But whereas her more famous classmate is associated with hard living, literary stardom, and an early, self-inflicted death, Janet Lewis embodies a very different path. She attended the University of Chicago, where she majored in French, and after her graduation left for Paris ("without waiting to pick up her diploma," one biographer notes), residing there for six months, not quite long enough to become enmeshed in the expatriate literary scene with which the city is so strongly associated.[7] Shortly after returning home she contracted tuberculosis, the disease that felled so many artists and nearly killed her as well. (Many years later, she told an interviewer, "There was a moment, be cheerful or die. You take your choice.")[8]

Despite the life-threatening illness in her youth, she went on to live an impressive ninety-nine years, most of those years in the same house in the hills of Northern California where she and her husband, the poet Yvor Winters, raised their two children. Her ability to balance her domestic life—by all accounts, she enjoyed a remarkably happy marriage—with decades of literary output gives her an image that is simultaneously traditional and feminist. In her book *Silences*, Tillie Olsen cites Lewis as a clear example of a talented woman writer whose literary production was inhibited by her obligations to family and to a more famous husband. Lewis acknowledged the challenges of balancing her familial responsibilities with her writing. "I do think those women who have turned out an enormous amount of work were generally not women who had children," she allowed in an early interview.[9] But at the same time she publicly and explicitly rejected Olsen's characterization of her, perhaps unwilling to see her family and her writing in conflict. "Being a writer has meant nearly everything to me beyond my marriage and children," she told an interviewer in 1983.[10] The remark is Lewis distilled. She foregrounds her marriage and her family. Beyond that, everything is about her writing.

As a poet, she met early success, publishing a four-poem sequence called "Cold Hills" in *Poetry* in 1920, before she had even finished college. A couple of years later, she moved into prose as well, publishing her first story in another influential magazine, *The Bookman*. Her first book of poems, *The Indian in the Woods*, was published in 1922 by the short-lived imprint Manikin, whose entire publishing history consists of three books: one by Lewis, one by William Carlos Williams, and one by Marianne Moore. It was just the beginning of a lifetime of close association with literary greatness, both personally and professionally.

A decade after her first book of poems, a period during which she got married and she and Winters both recovered from tuberculosis, she published her first novel, *The Invasion*, her first foray into historical fiction. Subtitled *A Narrative of Events Concerning the Johnston Family of St. Mary's*, it is set in the Great Lakes region and tells the story of an Irish immigrant who marries an Ojibway woman.

Almost ten years after that, she published her acknowledged masterpiece, *The Wife of Martin Guerre*, marrying her eye for history with the peculiarities of the legal system that would give her the platform from which to explore powerful questions of morality and personal responsibility that fuel the three *Cases of Circumstantial Evidence*.

To European critics, Lewis seems quintessentially American. To American critics, her fondness for European settings leads to comparisons as expected as Flaubert and as unusual as the Provençal writer Jean Giono. The *New York Times* compared her to Melville and to Stendhal. Another critic sees her, based on *The Invasion* and some of her short stories, as a definitive voice in Western regional writing. In some ways, Lewis's writing remains elastic, allowing other writers to see in her a powerful reflection of their own interests. Novelists claim her novels as her best work. Poets are drawn again and again to her diverse body of poetry, which attracts new requests for reprinting in anthologies every year. In short, as with all the best writers, her work and her decades-long career defy simple categorization or comparisons.

Despite Lewis's resistance to easy definitions, her many literary admirers, including Theodore Roethke, Wallace Stegner, and so many more, agree on two things: that her writing, particularly the poems and the historical novels, is first-class; and that she deserves a much wider readership. It is for exactly this reason that Swallow Press has created the present edition. But if Lewis herself felt neglected as an author, there is no evidence of it. In person and in published comments, she championed graciousness. She sent thank-you notes to our publishing offices here in Ohio upon receiving her yearly royalty check. Late into her nineties, she charmed literary pilgrims who found their way to her house in Los Altos, serving them tea and apologizing for the self-described "laziness" that led her to sleep until the late hour of 8:30 in the morning, and for the periods of quiet introspection that meant she would sometimes go for many years without publishing new work, only to pick up again in startling new directions, be it in writing opera libretti (she wrote six, including adaptations of her own *Wife of Martin Guerre* and James Fenimore Cooper's *The Last of the Mohicans*), or in poems quite different from the Imagist work with which she began her career.

Her disarming modesty, about her own character as well as her writing, is the most constant theme in interviews and profiles. This exchange, in the *Southern Review,* is characteristic:

> Interviewers: Many writers and critics—Evan Connell and Donald Davie, to name a couple—admire your work greatly. Yet, you are not widely known. What is your reaction to this?

> Lewis: I think I've had as much recognition as I need and probably as much as I deserve.[11]

She stated that her goal in writing her *Cases of Circumstantial Evidence* was equally modest: to stay as close to the history as possible and to let the characters and the facts speak for themselves. She demonstrated a similar sense of duty to her husband, the man who gave her the book that made these novels possible. For the thirty years that she outlived him, she kept their home in Los Altos much the way that it had been when he was alive, with his name on the mailbox and his writing shed maintained as if he might return, any moment, to use it.

It would have been impossible to predict the success of this modest professor's daughter, born at the very end of the nineteenth century. But her first poem in *Poetry*, which appeared at the height of modernism and when she was only twenty years old, seems to anticipate both her long life and the way her work stands on its own, just outside the literary canon. She writes,

> I have lived so long
> On the cold hills alone . . .
> I loved the rock
> And the lean pine trees,
> Hated the life in the turfy meadow,
> Hated the heavy, sensuous bees.
> I have lived so long
> Under the high monotony of starry skies,
> I am so cased about
> With the clean wind and the cold nights,
> People will not let me in
> To their warm gardens
> Full of bees.

Swallow Press is honored to be the bearer of Lewis's literary legacy, not just the three great novels but her collection of short stories and her books of poems—a lifetime of close witness to the public and the private, and a deep appreciation for the human condition.

Kevin Haworth
Executive Editor
Swallow Press

Notes

1. Robert McG. Thomas Jr, "Janet Lewis, 99, Poet of Spirit and Keeper of the Hearth, Dies," *New York Times*, December 5, 1998, 16.

2. Larry McMurtry, "The Return of Janet Lewis," *New York Review of Books* 45, no. 10 (1998): 24.

3. Roger Hofheins and Dan Tooker, "A Conversation with Janet Lewis," *Southern Review* 10, no. 4 (1974): 336.

4. McMurtry, 24.

5. Alan Swallow, *An Editor's Essays of Two Decades* (Seattle: Experiment Press, 1962), 334.

6. Janet Lewis, "Sources of *The Wife of Martin Guerre*," *TriQuarterly* 55 (Fall 1982): 105.

7. Charles L. Crow, *Janet Lewis* (Boise, ID: Boise State University, 1980), 9.

8. Mitzi Berger Hamovitch, "My Life I Will Not Let Thee Go Except Thou Bless Me: An Interview with Janet Lewis," *Southern Review* 18, no. 4 (1982): 307.

9. Crow, 11.

10. Marilyn Yalom, *Women Writers of the West Coast: Speaking of Their Lives and Careers* (Santa Barbara: Capra Press, 1983), 21.

11. Hofheins and Tooker, 341.

Foreword for the
First Swallow Press Edition

I first came upon the story of the wife of Martin Guerre in a collection called *Famous Cases of Circumstantial Evidence.* This volume contained, together with an essay, The Theory of Presumptive Proof, by Samuel March Phillips (1780–1862) (who in 1814 with the publication of his book *Phillips on Evidence* superseded Chief Baron Gilbert as an authority on the English law of evidence), many historic accounts of the failure of justice because of undue reliance on circumstantial evidence. Some of the cases presented occurred after the death of Phillips, and there is no way of knowing who recorded them, or from what sources. The trial of Martin Guerre, however, is described and discussed by the famous French jurist, Estienne Pasquier (1529–1615), in his extraordinary and encyclopedic work, *Les Recherches de la France.* Pasquier says: Maître Jean Corras, grand Jurisconsulte, qui fût rapporteur du procès, nous en representa l'histoire par escrit, avec commentaires pour l'embellir de poincts de droict. (Master Jean Corras, great jurist, who was the recorder for the trial, has presented us with the written story, with commentaries to embellish it in points of law.) It is reasonably certain that whoever wrote the story for the *Famous Cases* had recourse to the work of Maître Corras. It is said that Corras later became a famous judge, and that he was hanged in his scarlet robes after the massacre of St. Bartholomew in the excitement which spread from Paris to the provinces, and which died away only in October of that year, 1572, almost twelve years to a day after the execution of Arnaud du Tilh. I have been told, also, that Michel de Montaigne refers in one of his essays to the curious case of Martin Guerre, his contemporary. I regret that I cannot cite the number of the essay. Still, between Pasquier, Montaigne, and Maître Jean Corras, we can be sure that such a trial indeed took place; and in retelling the story of Bertrande de Rols I have tried to be as faithful to the historical events as the distances of time and place permit. The account of the trial by Pasquier is briefer than that in the *Famous Cases*, but contains a few interesting details not given in the latter. He concludes his account by these words: Mais je demanderois volontiers si ce Monsieur Martin Guerre qui s'aigrit si âprement contre sa femme, ne maritoit pas une punition aussi griefve qu'Arnaut Tillier, pour avoir par son absence esté cause de ce mesfait? (But I would willingly ask you if this Monsieur Martin Guerre who became so embittered toward his wife, did not deserve a punishment as severe as that of Arnaud Tillier, for having been by his absence the cause of this wrong-doing?)

J.L.

[1947]

The Wife of Martin Guerre

I. Artigues

One morning in January, 1539, a wedding was celebrated in the village of Artigues. That night the two children who had been espoused to one another lay in bed in the house of the groom's father. They were Bertrande de Rols, aged eleven years, and Martin Guerre, who was no older, both offspring of rich peasant families as ancient, as feudal and as proud as any of the great seignorial houses of Gascony. The room was cold. Outside the snow lay thinly over the stony ground, or, gathered into long shallow drifts at the corners of houses, left the earth bare. But higher, it extended upward in great sheets and dunes, mantling the ridges and choking the wooded valleys, toward the peak of La Bacanère and the long ridge of Le Burat, and to the south, beyond the long valley of Luchon, the granite Maladetta stood sheathed in ice and snow. The passes to Spain were buried under whiteness. The Pyrenees had become for the winter season an impassable wall. Those Spaniards who were in French territory after the first heavy snowfall in September, remained there, and those Frenchmen, smugglers or soldiers or simple travelers who found themselves on the wrong side of the Port de Venasque were doomed to remain there until spring. Sheep in fold, cattle in the grange, faggots heaped high against the wall of the farm, the mountain villages were closed in enforced idleness and isolation. It was a season of leisure in which weddings might well be celebrated.

Bertrande had not spoken to Martin in all her life until that morning, although she had often seen him; indeed she had not known until the evening before that a marriage had been arranged. That morning she had knelt with Martin before his father and then had walked with him across the snow, dressed bravely in a new red cape and attended by many friends and relatives and by the sound of violins, to the church of Artigues where the marriage ceremony had been completed. She had found it quite as serious an affair as first communion.

Afterwards, still to the music of the violins, which sounded thin and sharp in the cold air, she had returned to the house of her husband where a huge fire of oak logs garnished with vine-trimmings roared in the big fireplace, and where the kitchen, the principal room of the house, was set with improvised tables, long boards laid over trestles. The stone floor had been freshly strewn with broken boughs of evergreen. The sides and bottoms of the copper pans flashed redly with the reflection of the flames, and the air was rich with the good smell of roasting meat and of freshly poured wine. Underfoot the snow from the sabots melted and sank beneath the trodden evergreens. A smell of humanity and of steaming wool mingled with the odors of the food, and the room was incredibly noisy with conversation.

It was a gay, an important event. Everyone was intensely jubilant, but the small bride received very little attention. After the first embraces and compliments, she sat beside her mother at the long table and ate the food which her mother served her from the big platters. Now and again she felt her mother's arm steal warmly about her shoulders, and felt herself pressed briefly against her mother's breast, proudly and reassuringly, but as the feast proceeded her mother's attention became more engrossed with the conversation of the curé, who sat opposite, and of the groom's father, who sat upon her other side, and Bertrande, immune from observation in the midst of all this commotion which was ostensibly in her honor, looked about the room at her ease, and fed pieces of hard bread dipped in grease to the woolly Pyrenean sheep dog with the long curly tail who nosed his head into her lap from his place beneath the table. By and by, when the dishes of soup and roast had given way to the boiled chestnuts, cheese, honey and dried fruits, she slipped from her place and began quietly to explore the room.

Behind the table where she had been sitting the beds were ranged, end to end, the curtains of yellow serge drawn close, each one an apartment in itself. The child brushed between these curtains and the stout backs of the merrymakers, moving slowly toward the nearer corner of the room, where she stood, her back against a tall cupboard, and surveyed the scene. Across from her the blackened fireplace occupied at least a third of the wall, and the brightness of the leaping flames left the corners on either side in confused semi-darkness. In the middle of the wall to the right, however, she spied a door, and toward that she gradually made her way. It proved to be the entrance to a long cold corridor, from which doors opened into storerooms, rooms for the shepherds, and lighted only by a small window of which the wooden shutters were closed. Another person had taken refuge from the festivities in this corridor, and was intent upon undoing the bolts of the shutters. The half of the shutter folded back, a flood of sharp snowy sunlight fell into the corridor, and in its brightness she recognized Martin. She made a step forward, uncertainly, and Martin, hearing it, turned and advanced upon her, his hands outstretched and a fearsome expression on his long, young face. He had disliked being married, and, in order to express his dislike of the affair, and also to express the power of his newly acquired sovereignty, he cuffed Bertrande soundly upon the ears, scratched her face and pulled her hair, all without a word. Her cries brought a rescuer, her mother's sister, who rebuked the bridegroom and led the bride back into the kitchen, where she remained beside her mother until the hour when she was led by her mother and her mother-in-law into the Chamber, the room on the opposite side of the kitchen, where stood the master's bed, now dedicated to the formalities of the wedding.

Bertrande was disrobed and attired in night garments and a bonnet-de-nuit. Martin was brought in and similarly attired, and the two children were put to bed together in the presence of all the company. In deference to the extreme youth of the bridal couple, however, the serge curtains were not pulled, and a torch, fastened to the wall, was left blazing.

The company remained in the room for a time, laughing at jokes of a time-honored nature, while the two children lay very still and did not look at each other. By and by the merrymakers drifted into the kitchen, and last of all the father of Martin Guerre paused in the doorway to wish his children a formal goodnight. Bertrande saw his features, exaggerated in the flare of the torch, bent in an expression of great seriousness, and the realization that henceforth her life lay beneath his jurisdiction came suddenly and overwhelmingly to the little girl. The door closed behind him. The unglazed window was also closed, but between the leaves of the shutter a draft came which shook the flame of the torch. Otherwise the air was still and dead. The floor was bare, and the room was unfurnished save for a row of carved chests against the wall and the great bed in which she lay. She was tired and frightened. She did not know what Martin might not take it into his head to do to her. Presently she felt him stir.

"I am tired of all this business," he said, turning on his side and burrowing his head into his pillow. Soon his breathing became regular, and, without daring to move her body, Bertrande relaxed. She was safe. Her husband was asleep.

From her high pillow she watched the torch, as the flame wavered, and little particles of blazing lint detached themselves and fell, smoking, to the stone floor. One was long in falling; it clung, a blazing thread, making the flame of the torch irregular and smoky. Then it too dropped. The warmth of the flock bed began to enclose the small thin body in something like security, a feeling almost as good as that of being home again. The light of the torch seemed to go out. The child began to doze.

An hour or so later the door opened and a large figure entered, substantially clothed in ample folds of brown wool and coifed in white linen, and bearing a tray; and crossed with leisured tread to the bedside. Whether it was merely the sense of being observed, or whether the stone floor had resounded or the silver rattled a little on the tray, Bertrande awoke and, opening her eyes, looked up into the square, benevolent face and the pleasant brown eyes of a woman whom she recognized dimly as a part of the house of Guerre. But it was not the face of her mother-in-law, no, it was the face of the servant who had stood at the doorway as the bridal party had returned from the church.

"You are awake. That is well," said the woman, smiling. "I warrant, if the boy were eight years older he would not be sound asleep at such an hour."

She rested the tray on the bed, and, reaching across the body of Bertrande, shook Martin by the shoulder.

"Surely it is not already morning," said Bertrande.

"No, my dear, it is réveillon. I have brought you your little midnight feast."

"Oh," said Bertrande, "they forgot to tell me about it."

She sat up, looking a little dazed and worried. Without instruction she might not know what to do, she might do the wrong thing. Martin, roused, also sat up, and together they surveyed the tray.

"It is not a bad idea at all," said Martin, his voice foggy with sleep, and, strangely enough, perfectly good-natured.

"Eat," said the woman, beaming upon them. "You have had all the rest of the affair—you may as well enjoy now your little feast, just the two of you. I prepared it myself."

Thus urged, the children rubbed their eyes and fell to, while the woman stood by, her hands on her well-draped hips.

"It is all kinds of an affair, this getting married," she said as she watched the children. "Don't overlook the custard—it is my specialty. And by and by you will appreciate all that your parents have done for you. And meanwhile what peace there is and what friendship in the village of Artigues! You are a pretty little girl, Madame, a little thin, perhaps, but with the years the limbs grow rounder. A little more flesh and you will be altogether charming. And you have a fine, bright color in your cheeks. Look at her, Martin. She is even prettier now than she was at the church, when she was so pale with emotion."

Bertrande ate gravely, licking the yellow custard from the large silver spoon. This was more attention than she had received all day, and, moreover, it was the sort of attention that she could understand. The woman continued in a rich, comfortable voice:

"Take Martin now. He will not be a pretty man, but he will be very distinguished, like his father. There is a kind of ugliness which is very fine in a man. For the rest, I doubt not but that he will be capable of all that is required of a man."

She smiled upon them with no intention of hurrying them, and continued:

"Also, Martin, look at your wife—she has the lucky eyes, the two-colored eyes, brown and green, and the lucky people bring luck to those they love."

They finished everything upon the tray, even dividing amicably the last bit of pastry between them, and the servant departed with a final word of commendation. Madame Martin Guerre, born Bertrande de Rols, comforted by the inward presence of pastry and custard and by the wholesome unconcern of her husband, fell into a deep untroubled slumber. In the morning she returned to the house of her parents, there to await an age when she should be more fitted to assume her married responsibilities.

So began for the wife of Martin Guerre the estate which was to bring her so much joy and also such strange and unpredictable suffering.

For the present, life went on as usual. She had not gained in personal importance or in liberty by becoming the wife of Martin Guerre; indeed she had not expected to do so. Advantages there were, certainly, from the marriage, but for the present they were all for the two families of Guerre and de Rols; later, Martin and Bertrande would profit from the increased dual prosperity. The solemn ceremony in the church, the recollection of awakening at night to be served royally with delicacies shining on the family plate of les Guerre, receded, overshadowed by the multiplicity of the daily tasks that were her education.

The union of the house of de Rols and that of Guerre had long been considered. It had appeared to three generations as almost inevitable, so many were the advantages for both families to be expected from such an alliance. Three generations ago the matter had been practically settled, until a remark by the great-grandfather of Bertrande de Rols upset the plans of the great-grandfather of Martin Guerre.

"I have a nice little granddaughter whom I'm keeping for you," said the ancestor of Martin to old de Rols, affably, at the close of a conversation which had covered the extent of the mutual benefits which might result from a union between the two families.

"If you wish to keep her well," said the great-grandfather of Bertrande, humorously, "if you wish to keep her very well, my friend, you have only to salt her."

The great-grandfather of Martin regarded de Rols for a moment without speaking, but he was no longer affable.

"You wish to imply then, that she will be easy to keep. You imply that the suitors will not be many. You imply that I may salt her and cover her with oil, like the carcase of a chicken, and she well keep, eh, she will keep indefinitely!"

"My friend, I imply nothing of the sort," said the other old man, patiently. "I only like to have my little joke."

"Your joke," replied Martin's great-grandfather, "your joke is an insult." And he spat in the face of Bertrande de Rols' ancestor.

The negotiations for the marriage were discontinued, and not only that, but great-grandfather Guerre and all his mesnie, that is to say, his sons and daughters and their families, his uncles and aunts and their families, and all the servants whose families had been accustomed to serve these families of the house of Guerre, conceived and maintained an intense hatred of the mesnie of the house of de Rols, which was continued until the birth of Bertrande. Then, since the house of Guerre had rejoiced in the birth of a son but a short time previous, it occurred to the descendants of the jesting and offended great-grandfathers that the best and only way to end a feud of such long standing was to affiance the infants in their cradles. This was accordingly done, and peace was restored.

One should not judge too harshly the pride of the grandfather who was insulted by so mild a jest. As head of his family, the *cap d'hostal*, he carried great responsibilities; the safety and prosperity of all his household depended largely upon the strict obedience and reverence which he could demand from his children, his wife and his servants. From great responsibility arose great pride. No one questioned his right to be offended and no one hesitated to follow his example in hating the offender—offenders, one should say, because the deed of one man became immediately the deed of his family. It is perhaps surprising, however, that the feudal structure should have been maintained so strictly and upon so large a scale by these peasants of Artigues, for these peasants were closer to the *seigneur campagnard* whom the close of the sixteenth century saw coming into prominence than they were to the average peasant of the lowlands, whose families were sprung from the emancipated serfs of the middle ages. The crags and valleys of the Pyrenees were the cause of their prosperity and of their pride.

The hot mineral baths in the valley of Luchon, it is true, were on one of the direct routes from Spain into France, and it is said that the soldiers of Caesar stopped there to soak their battle-weary limbs in the muddy sulphur pools, but the court of Navarre neglected Luchon. The Marguerite of Princesses took her entourage to Cauterets, nearer Pau. Neither was Artigues upon the direct way through the valley of Luchon to the valley of the Garonne. It stood nearer to a small tributary to the Neste in a higher fold of the mountains. It was on the way to no other village. No one visited Artigues who had not business there. And so from generation to generation, while the lowland villages were plundered and burned and their fields laid waste by the religious wars which swept southern France through the thirteenth century and down to the middle of the sixteenth, Artigues enjoyed its isolation and its lack of fame, and actual gold accumulated in the coffers of its more prosperous families. The feudal feeling maintained its value also, as strong as in the earlier centuries, although Francis the First had been for twenty-one years upon the throne of France and although Languedoc had belonged to the French crown almost three hundred years.

When she was fourteen years of age, perhaps a little earlier than might have been the case had it not been for the death of her own mother, Bertrande de Rols went to live finally with the house of Guerre. One deceptively warm autumn forenoon, attended by the servant who had brought the réveillon to the young bridal couple, she crossed the courtyard, barefoot, dressed quite simply in her usual workaday clothes, and found herself on the threshold of the big kitchen. Her mother-in-law kissed her on both cheeks, and led her to the hearth. The wooden coffers which contained her personal effects and the linen and silver of her dowry were carried in and set against the wall, her mother-in-law indicated to her the large bed with the curtains of yellow serge which was to be hers and Martin's, and, without too great haste, she was set to grinding meal in a big stone mortar. Martin and his father were in the fields. Her own father had ridden off to oversee the vintaging. None of the field-workers returned until nightfall. But meanwhile she had time to become familiar with the kitchen, with Martin's four sisters and the servants, with the dogs and cats and with the feathered inhabitants of the basse-cour. She had not visited the house since the day of her wedding, but the scene was much as she had remembered it. The big table on trestles had been removed; there remained only a square table near the hearth, for the family, and a long one beside it for the workers. The floor was strewn only with dried grass, and the walls were not garnished with evergreen; but festoons of garlic and onions, the long stems braided together, hung from the rafters, together with bunches of dried elder blossoms and linden flowers. Bunches of dried rosemary, mountain thyme, and parsley were there also; and, in the hood of the chimney, meats and sausages were freshly hung to benefit from the resinous smoke.

Not again for a long time did Bertrande enjoy as much of her mother-in-law's attention as she did that afternoon, but the leisured kindness and interest which Madame Guerre bestowed upon her son's young wife threw a long warm shadow which extended forward for many days. She showed Bertrande the farm in detail, the stables, the granary, low stone buildings roofed with tile, like the house, set to the right and left of the courtyard before the house; showed her the room used for the dairy, the storerooms with their pots of honey and baskets of fruit, baskets of chestnuts, stone crocks of goose and chicken preserved in oil, eggs buried in bran, cheeses of goat's milk and of cow's milk, wine, oil. In the Chamber she showed her wool and flax for the distaff, the loom on which the clothing for the household would be woven. She showed her the garden, now being set in order for the early frost, the straw-thatched beehives, the sheepfold of mud and wattles, and last of all, returning to the Chamber in which the marriage bed had been dressed, Madame Guerre opened certain chests filled with bran and showed the young girl the coats of mail of the ancestors, thus preserved from rust. She did all this, as Bertrande well knew, that the young wife might understand the household which she would one day be called upon to direct. At no season of the year could she have summarized more happily all that the labors of the spring and summer were working to achieve.

The dusk came early with a chill that presaged winter. It was fully dark before the men began to assemble from the fields and pastures. The tables were set, and fresh bundles of vine trimmings were flung on the fire. The cattle were driven home and stabled, as was necessary every night in the year because of the depredations of bears. The sheep came next, their voices filling the courtyard with a high prolonged babble. The shepherd and the cowherd, entering the kitchen, brought the smell of the beasts into the room. The swineherd came next, and the men who were, turn and turn about, waggoners, vine dressers, or harvesters of grain. Last of all came the head of the family, Martin's father, squired by his son. His wife met him on the threshold with a cup of warmed wine, which he drank before he entered the house. He removed his cape and gave it to one of his daughters. He seated himself at the head of the table. The eldest daughter brought him a bowl of water and a napkin. He washed and wiped his hands, and then, searching the room with his eyes, found Martin's wife and signaled her to approach.

"Sit here, my daughter," he said, indicating a place beside him. "Tonight you shall be waited on. Tomorrow you shall have your own share of the labors of the house."

He did not smile, but the deed and the voice were kind. Bertrande, gazing cautiously into his face as his attention was directed elsewhere, now to the conversation of the shepherd, now toward the blazing hearth, remembered the severe paternal countenance as she had seen it by torchlight from the high pillow of the marriage bed, and she thought that the torchlight had changed it. Here, in the more even glow of the fire, the face of her new father held nothing terrifying. Seamed, coarsened by exposure to rough weather, the darkened skin caught the gold reflections squarely, without compromise or evasion, admitting all the engravures of time. The beard was short, rough and grizzled, parted to show a cleft in the long chin. The mouth, not smiling, but just, had a heavy lower lip which could admit of anger. The nose was short and flattened, the cheek bones were high, the forehead was high and wide, the eyes, now gray, now black, as the light changed, were calmly interested, calm in the assurance of authority. He sat at ease in the stiff-backed rush-bottomed chair, his dark jerkin laced to the throat, his right hand resting on the edge of the table, vigilantly surveying his household, like some Homeric king, some ruler of an island commonwealth who could both plow and fight, and the hand which rested on the table was scarred as from some defensive struggle in years long gone by. Without bearing any outward symbol of his power, he was in his own person both authority and security. He ruled, as the contemporary records say, using the verb which belongs to royalty, and the young girl seated beside him, in feeling this, felt also the great peace which his authority created for his household. It was the first of many evenings in which his presence should testify for her that the beasts were safe, that the grain was safe, that neither the wolves, whose voices could be heard on winter nights, nor marauding bands of mercenaries such as the current hearsay from the larger valleys sometimes reported, could do anything to harm the hearth beside which this man was seated. Because of him the farm was safe, and therefore Artigues, and therefore Languedoc, and therefore France, and therefore the whole world was safe and as it should be.

Martin was sufficiently kind to her, in spite of her apprehensions. He treated her with rather more affection than he did his sisters, bullying her occasionally, as he never bullied them, leaving her for the most part to her own affairs. At night they slept together in their own bed, shoulders turned away from each other, the tired young heads buried deep in the feather-stuffed pillows. Bertrande continued, day by day, her long apprenticeship for the position which she was destined to fill, that of mistress of the farm.

A year went by, during which Bertrande was aware of no other sentiment for her husband than a mild gratitude for his leaving her alone. Then, in the early autumn, Martin went bear-hunting. A cordon had been organized in the parish, according to custom, in order to check to some extent the increasing boldness of those animals which not only destroyed the young barley in the spring but also attacked cattle and sheep. It was generally maintained that there were two species of bear in the Pyrenees, those which were vegetarians strictly and those which were carnivorous. The latter were a far greater menace than the wolves, which were not seen in summer and which were dangerous only in the winter months when stock was likely to be safe in stable or fold. Martin had heard of the cordon, and, without saying anything to anyone, had risen early and gone off to join the hunters. He was not seen all that day. When evening came, the workers returned to the farm, shepherd, swineherd, carter, vintager, but no Martin. Monsieur Guerre inquired for his son, but no one had any information to offer. According to custom, the farm workers and the household servants sat down with their master while Madame Guerre and Bertrande waited upon them. The usual talk of the day's work went on, the meal was finished, the tables were cleared away, and the hour for prayers drew near, before the door burst open and Martin entered, staggering under a load of bearmeat done up in the yet bloody hide of the bear. He was exultant. But when he saw his father's expectant eyes, his exuberance died away, and, depositing his booty before his father, he made his excuses for being absent from the farm labor, and recounted, more briefly than he had intended, the adventures of his day. His father watched him quietly. When the boy had finished, his father said,

"That is all you have to say?"

"Yes, my father."

"Very well. Kneel."

Martin dropped on his knees, and his father, leaning forward, struck him with the knuckles of his right hand full upon the left side of his jaw. Martin said nothing. Madame Guerre caught her breath but made no outcry. In a moment Martin stood up and went to spit blood into the fire.

"Prayers, my children," said the father.

The household, upon its knees, with bowed heads, attended to the prayers which the father repeated, and then, dispersing, went off to bed. Several hours later that evening when the house was quiet and only a small gleam of firelight shone through the folds of serge which enclosed their bed, Bertrande said to Martin:

"Are you awake?"

"Certainly. My jaw aches. He has broken me two teeth."

"It was not just," she whispered with indignation.

"Certainly it was just. I didn't ask him if I might go. I was afraid that he might refuse me. But it was well done, was it not, to kill a bear?"

"Oh, yes," she replied fervently. "Martin, you are brave."

He said nothing to that, agreeing in his heart, but as he fell asleep, later, his arm rested on her shoulder. She had sided with him against the paternal authority, however just that authority might be. They were two, a camp within a camp. As for Bertrande, to her own surprise she began to understand that Martin belonged to her and that her affection for him was even greater than her respect and admiration for his father.

In the morning Madame Guerre, examining the damage done to her son's teeth, wept, but did not protest against her husband's severity.

"You understand, my son, it is necessary," she said. "If you have no obedience for your father, your son will have none for you, and then what will become of the family? Ruin. Despair."

"Yes, my mother, I understand," said Martin.

No one but Bertrande had hinted that the punishment was arbitrary and severe, and nothing further was said by anyone about the matter.

But gradually Bertrande's affection for her husband became a deep and joyous passion, growing slowly and naturally as her body grew. All about her, life flourished and increased itself, in field, in fold, in the rose-flushed bramble stems of spring before the green leaf unfurled, and in the vine leaves of autumn that lay like fire along the corded branches. She felt this passion within herself like the wine they drank in the early days of spring, light, tart, heady, and having a special fragrance, and her delight illuminated her love like the May sunshine pouring downward into the cupped wine. Early in her twentieth year she gave birth to a son, and her happiness seemed crowned and sanctified beyond anything she had ever dreamed. They called the boy Sanxi. His grandfather, receiving him in his arms a few minutes after his birth, rubbed his lips with garlic and touched them with a few sour drops of the wine of the country, welcoming him as a true Gascon. The boy thrived, and his mother thrived with him, as if they lent each other well-being.

Being the mother of an heir, Bertrande now received from her parents-in-law a new esteem which was manifest in little favors. This filled her with pride and contributed in no small measure to the grace with which she carried her dark head. More than ever she understood her position in the household, part of a structure that reached backward in time towards ancestors of whose renown one was proud and forward to a future in which Sanxi was a young man, in which Sanxi's children were to grow tall and maintain, as she and Martin now helped to maintain, the prosperity and honor of the family.

Martin had been placed in full charge of certain labors of the farm, and more especially in charge of certain fields.

He was responsible to his father for all he did, but the method and the details were in his own hands. It was a part of his progress toward the assumption of the full authority of the farm, which could not come to him until after his father's death, but for which he must be early prepared.

His situation was moreover curious in this respect; for the extent of his father's lifetime Martin would remain legally a minor. He might grow old, Sanxi might marry and have sons, but as long as the elder Guerre survived, so long was he absolute head of the house, and such liberty as Martin might enjoy was to be enjoyed only under his father's rule. This was so well understood together with the necessity for the law, that it never occurred to Martin to suppose it might be otherwise. It was known throughout Languedoc that a father owned the privilege of freeing his son, if he chose, from the parental authority, but this could only be done through a deliberate and formal ceremony; and although there were fathers who sometimes so liberated their sons, if anyone had asked Martin Guerre what he thought of such a procedure, he would almost certainly have replied that he thought ill. All such authority as belonged to the *cap d'hostal* Martin Guerre wished to retain, however much he might personally suffer for the time being under such authority. After the lapse of years he expected himself to be *cap d'hostal*, and when that responsibility should rest upon him he would have need of all the accumulated authority of antiquity, even as his father had need of it now.

Martin resembled his father greatly, both physically and in disposition. Bertrande, who sometimes observed his smothered resentment, or impatience at his inferior position, understood both the impatience and the attitude which kept it in control, the acceptance of things as they were, and said quietly to herself:

"In his day he will make a protector for this family as like his own father as two men well may be, and for that thanks to God."

Outwardly, Martin had the swarthy skin, the high forehead, the gray eyes, the flat, short nose, the lips, the high cleft chin of his father, and something of his father's build. Too early labor at the plow had rounded his shoulders. Nevertheless he was a skillful swordsman and boxer, agile, tall, and well-developed for his years. "Not a pretty man," as the servant had said, "but a very distinguished man." His ugliness was ancestral, and that in itself was good.

People so reasonable, so devoted, so strongly loving and hard working should have been exempt, one feels, from the vagaries of a malicious fate. Nevertheless, the very virtues of their way of life gave rise to a small incident, and from that incident developed the whole train of misfortune which singled out Bertrande de Rols from the peace and obscurity of her tradition.

It was a day in autumn. The vintage was done and the winter wheat was being put in the ground. Since the men were not expected to return to the farm at noon, Bertrande had taken Martin's lunch to him, and while he ate, she sat beside him on the sun-warmed, roughened earth at the edge of the field. She was bare-footed and bare-headed, the bodice of her gown open a little at the throat because of the noonday heat. The flesh at the edge of the gown was creamy, and the color deepened upward into a warm tan, growing richer and brighter on the rounded cheeks; and at the edge of the hair, in the shadow of the thick dark locks, the creamy color showed again, now moist from the sheltered heat. She watched her husband with tender, happy eyes. Before them, the cultivated ground slanted downward to a hazel copse. They could hear above them the murmur of the stream, reduced from its full summer flow, where it ran under the chestnut trees, before it circled the field, running below them through the copse and on into the narrowing valley. Across the valley and on the higher slopes, the beech and oak woods were tinged with gold and russet, and higher still a blue haze seemed to be gathering, like threads of smoke. Leaf, earth, and wine in the still sunlight gave forth the odors of their substances; the air was full of autumn fragrance. Martin, when he had finished his lunch, wrapped the fragments of bread and cheese and put them in his wallet. He returned the earthen wine jug to the hands of his wife and said:

"I am going away for a little while."

Bertrande made an exclamation of surprise.

"You may well be astonished," replied Martin. "This is the way of it. This morning I took from my father's granary enough seed wheat to plant the half of this field."

"You did not ask him for it?" cried Bertrande in alarm.

"Certainly, no. He would have denied it to me because it is his notion that I should put aside whatever grain I need from my own harvesting. But this year I have more land under cultivation than I had hoped to have. Should I let it go to waste? He has finished his planting; the wheat remains un-used. So I took it, and I have planted it. Was it not well done?"

"It was well done," she answered, "but I am afraid for you."

"I am afraid for myself," he said with a smile. "Without a doubt, he would flay me. Therefore I am going away. When he has had time to reflect, he will see that it was well done, and he will forgive me. Then I can return. You remember the bear?"

He rubbed his hand reminiscently along his jaw while Bertrande also smiled a little.

"You will have to be gone at least a week," she said. "Perhaps longer. If I could send you word . . ."

"Eight days should be enough," said Martin. "It is done for the good of the house—he will see that. And it is better that you should not know where I am in case he asks you. I shall go to Toulouse, then further, so that you can answer honestly, 'I do not know where he is.' Embrace my little son for me, and do not be disturbed."

She kissed him on both cheeks, feeling the warmth of the sun upon his flesh, caressing with her hand the short smooth beard, and then, in a brief premonition of disaster, held to his arm and would not let him go.

"Do not distress yourself," he repeated tenderly. "I shall be safe. I shall enjoy myself, moreover And I shall see you in a week."

So he went off. Once he turned to wave with a free, elated gesture, and then the shadows of the trees engulfed his figure. Bertrande returned to the farm, swinging the empty jug from a forefinger and thinking of the path which led down the valley beside the torrent falling and tumbling toward the Neste. Once she stepped aside to let pass a herd of swine being driven up into the oak forest to feed on acorns. She greeted the swineherd absently, thinking of Martin's journey, and how he would pass village after village, ford the cold streams, follow the narrow passes beside the Neste and eventually emerge into the greater valley of the Garonne, see the level fields, the walled cities, broad roads traversed by bands of merchants and armed men. The woods were still after the passage of the beasts—no insects and few birds. She wished that she might have gone with Martin. At the farm she found Sanxi, and was glad that she had not gone.

The afternoon passed as usual, but at suppertime, when Monsieur Guerre asked her where Martin was, and she answered, as had been arranged between them, "I do not know," she trembled beneath the cold gray gaze, penetrating and clear as a beam of light reflected from a wall of ice.

When it was learned that certain baskets of grain had been removed from the granary, the anger of Monsieur Guerre was terrible, as she had known it would be, and she was thankful that Martin's shoulders were beyond the reach of his father's heavy whip. At the end of a week the anger of Monsieur Guerre had not abated. Apprehensively Bertrande listened at the approach of every passer-by, started and turned cold each time the door to the house creaked on its broad hinges, and hoped that Martin might be fortunately delayed. Again and again she wished that some arrangement had been made between them by which she might meet and warn him. As week followed week, alarm at his prolonged absence began to mingle with the fear of his premature return. At the end of a month she was almost certain that some evil must have befallen him, and in great fear and agitation presented herself before the father of the family and confessed all that she knew of Martin's design.

Monsieur Guerre listened to her in silence, without moving a finger. Then he answered coldly:

"Madame, that my son should have become a thief is the greatest shame I have ever been asked to bear. Since he is my son, my only son, and since the welfare of the house depends upon the succession of an heir, I consider it my duty to forgive him. When he returns and confesses his crime, and has borne his punishment, I shall withdraw my anger. Until that time, no matter how distant it may be, rest assured, Madame, my anger shall exist. You may return to your work, Madame."

It was terrible to her to be addressed in this manner by a man whom she so greatly respected. "For their children," wrote the learned Etienne Pasquier a few years later, "fathers and mothers are the true images of God upon earth," and this was not an opinion which Pasquier imposed upon his time, but one in which he had been schooled. Bertrande admitted the inflexible justice of Martin's father, and regretted bitterly that she had fallen in with Martin's plans for avoiding punishment. How much better if he had stayed and submitted! He would now be forgiven and all would be well. She now prayed that he return at once. But the winter deepened about the village of Artigues, the ways were blocked with snow, and as even the mountain torrent became locked under ice she abandoned all hope of seeing him that winter.

It was lonely without him. The days, shortened by the double shadow of winter and of the steep mountain-sides, held little gaiety for the wife of Martin Guerre, and the nights were unutterably long. When spring came, the snow melted and all the valley was murmurous with the sound of rushing water. Still Martin delayed his return, and she said to herself:

"It is too early to hope for him. All the streams are flooded, the fords are impassable. Men and horses have been drowned trying to cross La Neste in flood."

She said this, but still her heart unreasonably demanded that he return and that quickly. With the first fine weather, the young wheat sprouting, the vines beginning to put forth tufts of silvery, crumpled leaves, with the half-wooded, half-cultivated valley ringing, now far, now near, with bird-song, her own youth and beauty quickened; and together with her consciousness of her youth, her beauty, her desire deepened for her husband. Somehow, with the winter, had died the fear that Martin might have been hurt or killed. She was at that time too young to believe in the reality of death. The reviving season held only her love and her impatience.

But spring went by, and Martin did not return. Through the deepening summer she looked for him in vain and only when the first heavy snow again closed the mountain passes did she admit to herself that her husband had left her. She knew that he had found the experience of liberty sweet, that to be master of his own actions was more precious to him than the society of his wife, the enjoyment of his son, or his share in the prosperity of the house. She believed that Martin was waiting until the time when he might return as head of the house, that he could not brook the idea of returning, not only to punishment, but to the continued rigors of his father's authority. She said nothing of this to anyone, but the thought was not an easy one to live with.

He had deserted her in the full beauty of her youth, in the height of her great passion, he had shamed her and wounded her, and when he returned, if he should return after the death of his father, his authority would be as great as his father's then was, and to murmur against his treatment of her would then be improper in the highest degree.

Martin's absence weighed upon the whole family. Although his father never mentioned his name, it was evident to those who knew him well that he had aged since Martin's departure. The second year after the disappearance of her son,

Madame Guerre died. She was not an old woman, and it may have been possible, as her daughters believed, that the illness from which she suffered during the last year of her life was greatly aggravated by the prolonged absence of her son. Bertrande assumed her duties and mourned her, for whatever their differences, always unexpressed by Bertrande, on other matters, the deserted wife had felt that her mother-in-law retained no anger against Martin. With Monsieur Guerre it was quite another matter. However perfect his courtesy to her, Bertrande felt always in his presence the just, inflexible displeasure that he maintained toward her husband, and she was reminded, also, that she had shared in Martin's plan. To his original offense, as time went by, Martin was also adding the greater offense of neglecting his inheritance.

The displeasure of Monsieur Guerre had become as necessary and inevitable a part of his character as his spine was of his body. When he entered a room that displeasure entered with him. The household, meanwhile, had changed and was no longer gay. Martin's elder sisters had married and lived elsewhere. The youngest, having married a cadet, or younger son, still lived at home and her husband had come to live with her. He was a quiet soul, deferring easily to Bertrande and to Monsieur Guerre. His presence did not greatly enliven the scene. Sanxi, who was excessively healthy, did not know how to be unhappy, and whether he played or rested, the place where he happened to be was for his mother the only joyous spot on the farm. For the rest, the household waited. Work went on, but the feeling of expectation was always in the air.

The fourth year after Martin's departure his father, though an expert horseman, was thrown from his horse, and, his head striking against a rock as he fell, he was killed instantly.

Bertrande, who had seen him ride away from the house, firm and erect in the saddle, could hardly believe the servants who came with the news an hour later. Still, there was something fitting in the manner of his death, which was abrupt, violent and absolute. The peremptory summons and the prompt obedience were like everything else in his way of living. It would have been difficult to conceive of him as grown old, yielding, little by little, perforce, his authority, hesitating and dwindling, and yet, if Martin had not returned, holding on to a life thoroughly exhausted in order not to leave the house without a master.

The shock of his death threw the family into confusion. Something like a panic seemed to overpower the servants and to reduce the four sisters of Martin to helpless children. And yet at the end of the day, Bertrande, finding for the first time a moment to herself, was surprised to consider how completely his death had been accepted, how long he seemed to have been dead who was not yet buried, whose death, early that morning, has been almost as remote as the day of judgment.

Pierre Guerre, the brother of Monsieur Guerre, had arrived in the afternoon and had announced his position as head of the family. He was a lesser man than his brother, shorter and broader of frame, with something of the family countenance but without the quality of great distinction that somehow had belonged to the old master. No less honest, but more simple, easier to approach, a good farmer, a solid soldier, Uncle Pierre had entered the kitchen and crossed with sober dignity to his brother's chair by the hearth. He had assigned tasks, taken the legal matters into consideration, sent for the priest and made public the news of the death. The

panic had subsided, the servants had gone about their business as usual, the older sisters had returned to their homes,
and Bertrande had said to herself:

"Now it will be safe for Martin to return."

She did not expect him to appear magically. She made
her own estimate of the time that it might take the news, trav-
eling uncertainly about the countryside, to reach him, and
how long it would take him to make the journey home. And
hope flourished and wore greener branches than in many a
long day. But as the year which she had allowed passed on
and drew to a close, her hope again declined, and there were
times when despair took its place entirely. She no longer had
the fine sense of immortality which she had felt before the
death of Martin's parents. Death had now become an actu-
ality rather than a possibility. Death was something that not
only could happen but that did happen.

A new fear assailed her. When she thought of Martin as
perhaps dead, his remembered features suddenly dissolved,
and the more she strove to recollect his appearance, the
vaguer grew her memory. When she was not trying to remember him, his face would sometimes reappear, suddenly
distinct in color and outline. Then she would start and tremble inwardly and try to hold the vision. But the harder she
tried, the dimmer grew the face. The same thing had happened to her, she now remembered, after her mother's death.
The beloved image had faded. An impression of warmth, of
security, the tones of the voice, the pressure of the hand had
remained, but she could not see her mother's face. She had
spoken of this to Madame Guerre, who had replied:

"There are people like that. They do not remember with
their eyes, but with their ears, maybe. With me, it is the eye,

and I could tell you at any moment in which chest I have laid away anything that you might want. I do not remember where it is, I see it. I cast my eye, as it were, over all my arrangements, and I see where I have laid the article which you desire."

Once indeed Bertrande thought that Martin had returned. She was walking on the path to the lower fields and was near the place where she had said farewell to her husband almost five years before. A man coming toward her under the shadow of the trees moved with Martin's gait and was so like him in build that Bertrande stopped, her hand on her breast and her heart leaping suddenly in such wild delight that she could hardly breathe. But the figure, approaching, lost its likeness to the man she loved. She saw presently that he was a stranger and that his features did not resemble those of Martin Guerre in the least. He did not even come near enough to pass her, but some few yards away turned off into the woods in the direction of Sode. Their eyes had met, like those of strangers who met in a narrow path, and he had saluted her, but without recognition.

After he had gone, she stood there, ready to weep in her sick disappointment. The day was cool, a day toward the end of winter, and she wore a heavy black wool cape with a hood, and on her feet were the pointed wooden sabots of her mountains, but she seemed to be standing barefoot on the moss, and bareheaded. Martin's hands were upon hers; she could see the familiar scars, the torn fingernail; and Martin's head was bent and touching hers. She could not see his face for his cheek was against her forehead. From the pressure of his hands upon hers such peace and joy flowed into her body that all the woods seemed warm, bathed in autumnal sunlight. The moment faded and she stood alone again in the thin winter air. She realized then that she had not seen his face, and wondered if that might be of good or bad omen. But the touch of his hand had been very living, and she renewed her hope.

If she heard of there being strangers in town, as there so often were, smugglers from Spain, or deserters from one army for another passing from kingdom to kingdom by way of the Port de la Venasque who delayed their wanderings to visit awhile in the rich mountain villages, she sent for them and entertained them overnight, giving them food, wine and a warm place to sleep. Of these she inquired for news of Martin. Had they, while serving with the Duke of Savoy or under the old Constable Montmorency or with the young Duke of Guise, heard of any man named Martin Guerre? Or bivouacked with him? Or perhaps fought by his side? None of these wanderers had met with such a man. They gave her, in return for her hospitality, other news, of how, before the death of the old king, Guienne, Angoumois and Saintonge had risen in insurrection because of the salt tax, of how at Angoulême the king's tax collectors had been beaten to death and sent "to salt the fish of the Charente," their flesh being flung into the river. She heard of the cruel revenge which Montmorency took under the new king, Henry, the second of that name, at Bordeaux, burning alive those who had killed the tax collectors, and oppressing and humiliating the whole city most grievously. She learned of the siege of Metz and of Henry's continuance of the quarrels of his father with the Emperor from men who had fought with Guise under the walls of that city. The Emperor had said, "I see now that Fortune is a woman; she prefers a young king to an old emperor," and, fatigued and ill, "his face all pale and his eyes sunk in his head, his beard as white as the snow," had made his resolve to abdicate and withdraw to Yuste, there on the other side of the Pyrenees in the Spanish monastery of the Cordeliers. Her imagination traveled far afield, thinking that wherever there was fighting, there Martin was likely to be; but of Martin himself she learned nothing. She charged these wanderers, upon their leave-taking, with a message to her husband, if they should chance to meet him:

"The old Master is dead. Come home."

She even made a journey once to Rieux, where her mother's sister then lived, thinking that to that town, which was a bishopric, almost as many travelers must come as to Toulouse. The town lay in a green meadow in a curve of the Arize, near to the spot at which that turbulent stream hurls itself into the Garonne. Behind it stood the wall of the Pyrenees. The delicate, bold spire of the cathedral, rising above the tiled roofs of the houses, seemed less tall than it was because of the height of the mountains. At the inn and at the cathedral doors Bertrande made her inquiries, and besought her aunt to question travelers whenever she might have the opportunity. She also begged that the death of Martin's father be announced from the cathedral. But a nostalgia came upon her there—she had never before left the parish of Artigues. She missed Sanxi, and everything seemed strange. Even the room in which she slept in her aunt's house seemed turned around, and the sun rose in the west and shone through western windows all the morning. Or so it seemed to Bertrande. After a few days she made her excuses to her aunt, and went home to Artigues.

And time went by. Meanwhile Sanxi, who in his earliest infancy had given some slight promise of growing to look like his father, daily grew more and more to resemble the sisters of

Martin Guerre, who had their mother's features and proportions rather than those of their father. This was at first a grief to Bertrande, although in considering Sanxi with his fresh young face and thick smooth chestnut hair, he seemed to her so altogether remarkable and charming that she could not wish him otherwise in any detail. She began to listen instead for the tones of his father's voice in the boy's light treble. So, nourishing her devotion with hope and with imagination, she took charge of Martin's household, tended his child, and waited.

The house flourished, Sanxi grew, and Bertrande increased in beauty. Her sorrow and her new sense of responsibility ennobled her physical charm. She acquired unconsciously a manner of gracious command. Eight years after the departure of her husband she no longer had the first tender radiance which had so pleased the young man, but a greater and more mature beauty had taken its place.

Eight years after the departure of Martin Guerre, Bertrande his wife was seated in the Chamber instructing her son in the catechism. The first warm days of summer were come, and neither mother nor son was paying as great attention as might have been paid to the lesson in hand. The room, large, dusky, cool, shut them effectively from the affairs of the kitchen and the courtyard. The wooden shutters were opened wide, but the window was high. It let in the sunshine but did not permit a view of the yard. The peace of the summer day without, the quiet half hour alone with Sanxi, the release from the continual round of practical duties had relaxed Bertrande. She looked at Sanxi's cool young cheek beside her knee and thought, "At last I begin to be at peace."

And her thought, sweeping backward quickly over all the moments of anguish, of desire, of hatred, even, hours of fierce resentment against Martin for making her suffer, for holding her from any other life than a prolonged fruitless waiting for his return, hours of terror when she had contemplated his death in some engagement of the Spanish wars, hours to be remembered with horror in which she had desired his death that she might be free of the agony of incertitude—all these reviewed in a moment with a sharp inward knowledge of herself, her thought returned like a tired dove to this moment of peace in which love was only love for Sanxi, as innocent and cool and gentle as the curve of his cheek. She regarded him thoughtfully and tenderly, and Sanxi, lifting his eyes to hers, smiled with a secret amusement.

"Repeat the answer, my son," said Bertrande.

Sanxi did so, his delight deepening.

"But you have given me that reply for two questions, Sanxi. You do not attend."

"No, mother, for three questions, the same answer," said Sanxi, suddenly hilarious.

"You must not make fun of sacred things," she said to him as gravely as she could, but neither of them was deceived, and as they smiled at each other, a hubbub arose in the courtyard which made Sanxi run to the window. Standing on his tiptoes, he still could not see much but the adjoining buildings. The tumult increased, with shrill cries, definitely joyous. Bertrande de Rols turned toward the door, leaning slightly forward in her chair. The noise, advancing through the kitchen, was approaching the Chamber, and suddenly the door swung open to admit Martin's Uncle Pierre, his four sisters and a bearded man dressed in leather and steel, who paused on the threshold as the others crowded forward. Behind him all the household servants and one or two men from the fields showed their excited ruddy faces. The old housekeeper, pushing past him, almost beside herself with joy, curtsied as low as she could, and cried:

"It is he, Madame!"

"It is Martin, my child," said Uncle Pierre.

"Bertrande," cried the sisters in chorus, "here is our brother Martin!"

Their voices filled the room, echoing from the low beams and the stone walls; they were all talking at once, and, as Bertrande rose to her feet, keeping one hand on the back of the chair to steady herself against a sudden, quickly passing dizziness, the bearded figure advanced gravely, surrounded by the agitated forms of the sisters, the uncle, the servants, who were now all swarming in behind the original group.

It was dark at the far end of the room. Bertrande stood in the sunlight and met, as in a dream, the long-anticipated moment, her breath stilled and her heart beating wildly. The figure in leather and steel advanced with even tread, a stockier figure than that of the man who had gone away eight years before, broader in the shoulder, developed, mature. The beard was strange, being rough and thick, but above it the eyes were like those of Martin, the forehead, the whole cast of the countenance, like and unlike to Bertrande's startled recognition, and as he advanced from the shadow he seemed to Bertrande a stranger, the stranger of the wooded pathway, then her loved husband, then a man who might have been Martin's ancestor but not young Martin Guerre.

When he had advanced to within a few feet of her, he stopped, and she read in his eyes a surprise and an admiration so intense that her limbs seemed all at once bathed in a soft fire. She was frightened.

"Madame," said the stranger who was her husband, "you are very beautiful."

"Cap de Diou!" exclaimed the uncle. "Are you surprised that your wife is beautiful?"

"Beautiful, yes, I knew, but beauty such as this I did not remember."

"Yes, Martin, yes," cried the sisters. "She has changed, you are right. It is another beauty."

"But why do you stand there? Embrace her, my nephew."

And then Bertrande felt on her cheek the imprint of the bearded lips, and on her shoulders the weight of the strong hands, felt with a shock the actual masculinity of the embrace, so strange for one who had been long accustomed only to the light touch of Sanxi's mouth. The embrace released her from her trance, reminding her of the last kiss which she had given Martin at the edge of the wheat field, and all the emotion tightly held in check for so many years was in her voice as she cried:

"Ah, why have you been away so long! Cruel! Cruel! I have almost forgotten your face! Even your voice, Martin, is strange in my ears."

"Bertrande," said Pierre Guerre with gravity, "this is no proper welcome for your husband, to overwhelm him with reproaches. You forget yourself, my child, indeed you do. My nephew, you must pardon her. It is the excess of emotion. We cannot tell you how we rejoice at your return. It was the greatest of sorrows to your father that you were gone so long. But that is over. I praise God that you are safely with us, no longer a boy, but a man grown. In times like these a house has need of a master and a child of a protector."

"I praise God also," said Bertrande softly, "and I ask your pardon, my husband."

"No, Uncle," came the reply. "She does well to reproach the man who left you all so long unprotected. It is I who should ask pardon of her. But you must believe me: until I passed through Rieux I did not know that my father was dead." And, bending above her hand, he promised Bertrande that he would never again leave her and that he would do all in his power to atone for the neglect which he had shown her. Bertrande was deeply touched and not a little surprised. Uncle Pierre remarked:

"It is well done, my nephew. I can see that the wars have done more for you than strengthen bone and muscle. You have spoken like a true father and like the head of a house "

Behind him the four sisters of Martin were agitated by murmurs of approval, and there were cries of approval and admiration from the servants, who, crowding forward, all wished to salute their long-absent master.

He greeted them all, inquiring for certain ones who had died during his absence, questioned them about their families and their health, praised them for their loyalty and good service, and appeared so genuinely pleased to see them all that their enthusiasm redoubled.

Bertrande, watching him, said to herself:

"He is noble, he is generous, he is like his father again, but become gracious."

But suddenly the master, putting aside gently the servants who stood between him and Bertrande, cried:

"But where is Sanxi? Where is my son, that I may embrace him?"

At this Sanxi, who had been hiding behind his mother, burrowed his head into her skirts, drawing the ample folds about his shoulders.

"Come, Sanxi," said his mother, taking him by the shoulders. "Here is your father, your good father of whom we have talked so many times. Salute him."

"Ah, my little monsieur," exclaimed a great voice, "it is good to see you," and Sanxi, clinging like a kitten to his mother's skirts, so that she had to disengage his fingers one by one, felt himself hoisted into the air and then folded close to a hard shoulder, smelt the reek of leather and horse-sweat, and then felt the wiry beard rubbed joyously against his face.

"Mama!" he cried. "Mama!"

"It is the strangeness," he heard his mother's voice saying apologetically. "Do not hold it against him. Consider, how sudden and how strange—for him, as for me."

"Tonnèrre!" cried the great voice. "He is hard to hold. But never mind. We shall be friends, in time."

The boy felt himself set on his feet firmly, and then his parents turned away from him. Some people pushed in between him and his mother, and as the crowd moved toward the door, everyone laughing and talking, it carried her along, clinging to the arm of the stranger. The swineherd and the boy who cared for the horses were the last to leave the room. They lagged behind, buffeting each other out of sheer good will, and the swineherd, turning, saw young Sanxi still standing in front of his mother's chair.

"What a fine day for you," he called. "It isn't everyday that a boy gets a father."

An hour later Sanxi had recovered himself sufficiently to dare sit beside his father on the long bench before the fireplace. On the other side of his father was the priest; in front of him, on a stool, was Uncle Pierre. His mother kept coming and going from the table to the fireplace, pausing sometimes with her hand on the shoulder of Uncle Pierre to gaze happily and incredulously at his father.

Uncle Pierre had to tell again how he had met Sanxi's father, "away by the church, far from the road to the farm. I knew him at once, and that from the back of his head. I cried, 'Hollah, Martin, my nephew, where are you going, away so far from your own house? You have returned,' I said. 'Pray do not leave us before you have seen your own roof.' And what answer did he make, this excellent man? 'I am going,' said he, 'to the church to give thanks to God for my safe return and to pray for the soul of my father of whose death I learned only yesterday.'"

The priest nodded with grave approval; the uncle wiped an actual tear from his eye.

"So then I cried, 'Good boy, embrace me, Martin, embrace your old Uncle Pierre,' and together we went and knelt in the church. I am glad that I have lived to see this day."

Then Sanxi's father had to hear from the priest and from Uncle Pierre all the story of how Sanxi's grandfather had fallen from his horse and been killed instantly, and of how his grandmother had died very quietly in her bed with all her family and her servants round about, weeping, all save her son Martin, and through all these recitals Sanxi was puzzled to see how his mother alternately wept and smiled. His father did not cry. He was very serious, very serious and strong, and Sanxi, sitting beside him, observed minutely all the straps and buckles of his armor and how the metal of his gorget had chafed the leather of his jerkin, and began to admire him, silently.

For the rest of the day he attached himself to his father's person, like a small dog who does not mind whether he is noticed or not, provided he is permitted to be present. He heard his father's brief account of his wanderings. He listened to the servants as they poured out to his father their stories of everything that had taken place since his departure, eight years ago. He even listened unnoticed while Uncle Pierre went over the business of the house with his father. And in the evening there were violins and flutes, roast meat as if it were a fête day, and neighbors riding in from miles around to welcome his father home. Sanxi had not known that his own household could be so gay. The very walls of the kitchen were animated and seemed to tremble in the ruddy glow from the chimney. The copper vessels winked and blazed. The glazed pottery on the dresser also gave back the quivering light, and his father's armor, as he flung himself back in his chair, or rose to meet a newcomer, was momentarily like the sky of an autumn sunset. But the seasons are tyrannical for the farmer. In the morning the flutes and violins were put away, and before dawn the men were about the usual work of the farm. The master to the fields, the mistress to the dairy—everything was just as usual until evening, and then, after supper before the hour for prayers, there was much talk by the fireplace of foreign lands, sieges and marches, the slaying of heretics, and finally, instead of his mother saying, "Prayers, my friends," there was the master of the house, like Sanxi's grandfather, announcing,

"My children, it is time for prayer."

The estate prospered surprisingly after the return of the master. The vigor of the man was contagious, and he had a way of noticing the work that a servant was doing and saying a word of approval that the old master had never had. For Bertrande, as for Sanxi, it was a new life, almost a new world.

Gladly she surrendered the responsibilities of the farm to her husband's care, and surrendered herself to his love. From having been a widow for eight years, she was suddenly again a wife. The loneliness of the house was dissipated. Even when there were not old friends come from a distance to greet Martin Guerre, even when the priest was not established in the corner of the hearth to hear accounts of the world below the mountains, there was good conversation in the house, and sometimes music, and Sanxi flourished and grew manly in the companionship of a hero. His newly-found father was no less to him.

At the end of a few months Bertrande found herself with child. She rejoiced thereat, and she also trembled, for at times a curious fear assailed her, a fear so terrible and unnatural that she hardly dared acknowledge it in her most secret heart. What if Martin, the roughly bearded stranger, were not the true Martin, the one whom she had kissed farewell that noonday by the side of the freshly planted field? Her sin, if such indeed were a fact, would be most black, for had she not experienced an instinctive warning? On the night of his return, overcome by desire and astonishment, she had trembled in his embrace and murmured again and again:

"Martin, it is so strange, I cannot believe it to be true."

To which the bearded traveler had replied:

"Poor little one, you have been too long alone."

In the morning her fear had vanished, Martin's family and friends, the servants, the very animals of the place, it seemed, affirming his identity, and putting her heart at peace.

So she had been happy, and had rejoiced in the presence of this new Martin even more than in that of the old, and it was not until she began to feel the weight of the child in her body that the fear returned. Even so, it did not stay. It was like the shadow of a dark wing sweeping suddenly across the room, and then departing swiftly as it had come, leaving all things standing as usual under the cold, normal light of day. But one day, seeing Martin returning from a ride with Sanxi, and seeing the easy comradeship between the two, she said aloud:

"It is not possible that this man should be Martin Guerre. For Martin Guerre, the son of the old master, proud and abrupt, like the old master, could never in this world speak so gaily to his own son. Ah! unhappy woman that I am, so to distrust the Good God who has sent me this happiness! I shall be punished. But this is also punishment in itself."

No one heard her speak, and, weeping bitterly, she withdrew to her own room where she remained until a servant came to find her at the hour of the evening meal. Nevertheless, in spite of her contrition, she could not refrain, the moment that they were left alone that evening, from accusing her husband of being other than the man he represented, and of asking for proof of his identity.

She had expected passionate proof or passionate denial. The man before her regarded her gravely, even tenderly, and said:

"Proof? But why proof? You have seen me. You have felt the touch of my lips. Behold my hands. Are they not scarred even as you remember them? Do you remember the time my father struck me and broke my teeth? They are still broken. You have spoken with me; we have spoken together of things past. Is not my speech the same? Why should I be other than myself? What has happened to give you this strange notion?"

Bertrande replied in a barely audible voice:

"If you had been Martin Guerre you would perhaps have struck me just now."

He answered with gentle surprise:

"But because I struck you on the day we were married, is that a reason I should strike you now? Listen to me, my dearest. Am I who speak to you now more different from the young man who left you, than that young man was different from the child you married?"

"When you left me," said Bertrande, "you resembled your father in flesh and spirit. Now you resemble him only in the flesh."

"My child," said her husband, ever more gravely, "my father was arrogant and severe. Just, also, and loving, but his severity sent from home his only son. For eight years I have traveled among many sorts and conditions of men. I have been many times in danger of death. If I return to you with a greater wisdom than that which I knew when I departed, would you have me dismiss it, in order again to resemble my father? God knows, my child, and the priest will so instruct you, that a man of evil ways may by an act of will so alter all his actions and his habits that he becomes a man of good. Are you satisfied?"

"And then," said Bertrande, in a still smaller voice, marshaling her last argument, "Martin Guerre at twenty had not the gift of the tongue. His father, also, was a silent man."

At this her husband, hitherto so grave, burst into a laugh which made the Chamber echo, and still laughing, with his broad hand he wiped the tears from her wet face.

"My darling, how funny you are," he said. "Weep no more. Every Gascon has the gift of the tongue. Some employ it, some do not. Since I am become no longer arrogant and severe, I choose to employ my gift." Then, more gently, he continued. "Madame, you are demented. It happens sometimes to women who are with child. Pay no attention to it. It will pass, and when your time is over, you will look back to this with astonishment."

"Perhaps that is it," said Bertrande in acquiescence. "For God knows I do not wish you to be otherwise than my true husband. When I went to visit my aunt in Rieux, being in a strange town, I became confused as to the directions, and not until I left that house did it seem to me, when I was within doors, that the east was not the west. So it must be with me now. For when I look at you it seems to me that I see the flesh and bone of Martin Guerre, but in them I see dwelling the spirit of another man."

"When I was in Brittany," said her husband, "I heard a strange story of a man who was also a wolf, and there may also have been times when the soul of one man inhabited the body of another. But it is also notorious that men who have been great sinners have become saints. What would become of us all if we had no power to turn from evil toward good?"

And so he led her on to talk of other matters, of foreign lands and battles in Flanders until she was again calm. She put her fear away, or rather, she regarded it as a delusion, and she gave herself over to the happy anticipation of her second child. In her affection for her husband was now mingled a profound gratitude, for he had delivered her, at least for the present, from the terror of sin. When, upon a certain day she asked him if he remembered such and such a little incident, and he responded, smiling, "No, and do you remember when I told you that your eyes are speckled like the back of a mountain trout?" she only smiled in return, full of confidence and ease.

"You did not say such things when you were twenty," she replied.

It was the time of year when the grapes were being harvested, and the odor of ripe muscats was in the air. When the wine was made and the leaves on the vine stocks had turned scarlet, Bertrande rode out among valleys that dipped in fire toward Luchon between the irregular advances of the woods, saw the conical haystacks burning with dull gold beside the stone walls of farm buildings, felt, as she rode in the sunshine, the cold invigorating sweep of wind from the higher mountains, lifted her eyes and saw how the white clouds piled high above the rich green of the pine woods and how the sky was intensely blue beyond, blue as a dream of the Mediterranean or of the Gulf of Gascony. And returning, toward evening to her own house, as the blue haze of evening began to intercept and transmute the shapes of things, she smelled the wood smoke from her own hearth fire and thought it as sweet as the incense which was burned in the church at Artigues. Or she saw at the far end of a field, a man wearing a scarlet jerkin working in a group of men uniformly clothed in brown, a small dot of scarlet moving about on long brown legs against the golden surface of the earth, and these things, intensely perceived as never before since she could remember, filled her with a piercing joy. The cold metallic gleam of halberds moving forward under a steely sky against the background of the russet woods, as a band of soldiers passed her by; the very feel and pattern of the frost upon the threshold early in the morning as the season advanced; the motion and songs of birds, until their numbers diminished; and then the iron sound of the church bell ringing in somber majesty across the cold valleys—all these she noticed and enjoyed as never before. And even, when winter had closed around them, one night from a far-off hillside, the crying of wolves had filled her with a pleasure enhanced with dread, for the doors were safely closed and all the animals safe within walls, and a good fire roared in the great fireplace, spreading shifting constellations of gold against the black throat of the chimney, so that the dread was a luxury, and her enjoyment of the strange distant voices all the greater. And all this vividness of feeling, this new awareness of the life around her, was because of her love for this new Martin Guerre, and because of the delight and health of her life-giving body. Yet even this love was intensified, like her pleasure in the cry of the wolves, by the persistent illusion, or suspicion, that this man was not Martin.

The illusion, if such it was, did not pass away at the termination of her pregnancy, as he had prophesied it would do, but she had grown used to it. It lent a strange savor to her passion for him. Her happiness, and the happiness of her children, especially that of the newly born, the son of the new Martin, shone the more brightly, was the more greatly to be treasured because of the shadow of sin and danger which accompanied it. She wrapped the little body in swaddling bands, sheltering the little bald head from the chill spring air with her softest woolen cloth, and walked out into the fields along paths still wet from melting snow, where the earliest spring blossoms had already pricked the dead leaves. The winter wheat showed its point of new sharp green, and the air alternately misted, showered, and shone in confusing variability.

In June the wheat was harvested and the brook of the valley was turned loose by irrigating ditches upon the stubble fields, which had already begun to parch and burn in the midsummer heat. The steep fields, being so flooded, were like a series of cascades and terraces, running and shining; yet the water also sank deep into the rich earth and before long the fields were bright, some with flowers and grass, some with the new crop of buckwheat. And still the happiness of Bertrande continued, accompanied always by the shadow of her suspicion, and she could no longer say:

"It will pass when I am delivered of the child."

Through the summer, little by little the shadow increased in the mind of Bertrande. In vain did she contend with it. In a thousand small ways her suspicion was strengthened, in ways so small that she was ashamed to mention them. She thought of speaking of the matter in confession, but checked herself, saying:

"The priest will think me mad." She did not say, "Or worse, he will find a way to prove that which I only suspect."

But this was in her mind, and day after day she turned aside, she doubled her tracks, like a pursued creature, trying to avoid the realization which she knew was waiting for her. But as time went on she found herself more and more surely faced with the obligation of admitting herself to be hopelessly insane or of confessing that she was consciously accepting as her husband a man whom she believed to be an impostor. If the choice had lain within her power she would undoubtedly have chosen to be mad. For days and weeks she turned aside, as in a fever, from what she felt to be the truth, declaring to her distracted soul that she was defending the safety of her children, of her household, from Uncle Pierre down to the smallest shepherd, and then at last, one morning as she was seated alone, spinning, the truth presented itself finally, coldly, inescapably.

"I am no more mad than is this man. I am imposed upon, deceived, betrayed into adultery, but not mad."

The spindle dropped to the floor, the distaff fell across her knees, and though she sat like a woman turned into stone and felt her heart freezing slowly in her bosom, the air which entered her nostrils seemed to her more pure than any she had breathed in years, and the fever seemed to have left her body. She began then quietly to array before her in this clear passionless light the facts of her situation as she must now consider it, no longer distorted through fear or shame or through the desire of the flesh. She knew that she would never again be able to pretend that this was the man whom she had married. Although she had loved him passionately and joyously, and perhaps loved him still, and although he was the father of her son, she must rid herself of him. But could she rid herself? If she asked him to go, would he go? If she were to accuse him publicly of his crime, could she prove it? And if she could not prove it, in bringing such an accusation would she not be wronging the entire family from Sanxi and herself to the least of the cousins and cousins-in-law? And what of her youngest son, the son of the impostor? Had he no claim upon her, that she should of her own free will dishonor his birth? Terror assailed her lest she be trapped inescapably, and in her profound agitation and fear she rose and paced back and forth in the long, silent room until she was fatigued and trembling. She crossed to the window, and, leaning on the high sill, looked down into the courtyard.

Dusk was gathering, an autumn dusk. The paving stones were black with damp, but by morning they would be lacy white. While she stood there, looking down, her husband rode into the yard. A boy ran to meet him, and led his horse away after he had dismounted. The smith, whose fire glowed dimly in the cold gray light, left his work for a moment to salute his master, and returned to his work, smiling and rubbing his blackened hands together; and the old housekeeper, she who had brought the réveillon to the child bride and groom, so many years ago, appeared on the doorstep, holding a cup of warm wine. The master paused on the threshold to drink the wine and thank the old woman, and Bertrande could see quite plainly the look of adoration with which she received the empty cup.

"How firmly he is entrenched," she sighed. "How firmly."

The next day, an occasion presenting itself as Martin's younger sister was praising his conduct to his wife, Bertrande ventured:

"Yes, he is very kind, very gentle. One would almost say, is this the same man who so resembled in action and in feature your father?"

"One would almost say so," assented the sister amiably.

"But I do say so," returned Bertrande. "Often I ask myself, can this man be an impostor? And the true Martin Guerre, has he been slain in the wars?"

"Mother of Heaven," replied the sister, shocked, "how can you say such a thing, even think so? It is enough to tempt the saints to anger. Oh, Bertrande, you have not said such a thing to anyone else, have you?"

"Oh, no," she answered lightly.

"Then for the love of Our Lady, never speak of it again to me or to anyone. It is unkind. Martin could consider it an insult. He might be very angry if he heard it."

"Very well," said Bertrande. "I was jesting," and she smiled, but her heart was sick.

At confession, kneeling in the stale, cold semi-darkness, her hands muffled in her black wool capuchon, her head bowed, she said, as she had long meditated but never dared:

"Father, I have believed my husband, who is now master of my house, not to be Martin Guerre whom I married. Believing this, I have continued to live with him. I have sinned greatly."

"My child," replied the voice of the priest, without indicating the least surprise, "for what reason have you suspected this man not to be the true Martin Guerre?"

"Ah, he also has suspected him," said Bertrande to herself, and her heart gave a great leap of joy, like that of an imprisoned animal who sees the way to escape.

She replied to the priest as she had replied to her husband, giving instances of his behavior which seemed to her unnatural.

"What shall I do," she besought him finally, "what shall I do to be forgiven?"

"Softly, my child," said the calm voice of the priest. "It is then for his kindness to you that you accuse him?"

"Not for his kindness, but for the manner of his kindness."

"No matter," said the priest. "It is because of a great change in his spirit. He spoke to me of this long since, being concerned for you, and it seems to me that he has been toward you both wise and gentle. Go now in peace, my daughter. Be disturbed no more."

Bertrande continued to kneel, only drawing her cloak closer about her shoulders. The cold air seemed to draw slowly through the meshes of the wool and rise from the cold stones on which she knelt. At last she replied incredulously:

"You then believe him to be no impostor?"

"Surely not," said the easy voice of the priest, warm, definite and uncomprehending. "Surely not. Men change with the years, you must remember. Pray for understanding, my daughter, and go in peace."

Slowly she got to her feet and slowly made her way through the obscurity to the doorway, pushed aside the unwieldy leather curtain, stepped outside into the freely moving air and the more spacious dusk, and descended the familiar steps. Familiar figures passed her, greeting her as they went on into the church. She answered them as in a dream, and as in a dream took the path to her farm. She felt like one who has been condemned to solitude, whether of exile or of prison. All the circumstances of her life, the instruction of the church, her affection for her children and her kindred rose up about her in a wall implacable as stone, invisible as air, condemning her to silence and to the perpetuation of a sin which her soul had learned to abhor. She could not by any effort of the imagination return to the happy and deluded state of mind in which she had passed the first years since the return of her husband. The realization that she was again with child added to her woe, and the weight, such as she had carried before in her body joyously, now seemed the burden of her sin made actual and dragged her down at every step.

The path, turning to follow the contours of the mountainside, brought her after a time to the crest of a slope above her farm. There it lay, house, grange and stable, set about with its own orchards, its chimney smoking gently, infinitely more familiar, more her own after all these years than the house in which she had been born; yet as she looked down toward it from the hillside she thought that it was no longer hers. An enemy had taken possession of it and had treacherously drawn to his party all those who most owed her loyalty and trust. Her eyes filled with tears, and when she drew her hands away from her face, a commotion had arisen in the courtyard below. People were running about with torches, gathering into a group from which excited cries, staccato and sonorous, rose toward the hillside, and presently three figures on horseback detached themselves from the group and rode away, the hoofs ringing on the stones. She remembered then that Martin had promised to make one of a cordon for a bear hunt from the parish of Sode, and knew that these must be his neighbors come for him.

When she reached her doorway, the housekeeper greeted her.

"The Master is gone to Sode. Ah, they are fortunate to have him! He is famous as a hunter of bear." She laughed, helping Bertrande to remove her cape; and did not see that her mistress's face had been stained with tears.

The next evening as they sat together, her husband said to Bertrande:

"Why do you look at me so strangely with your lovely two-colored eyes, your lucky eyes?"

"I was wondering when you would leave me to return again to the wars."

"I have told you never, never until you cease to love me."

"I have ceased to love you. Will you go?"

Something in the quality of her voice restrained the man from jesting. "I do not believe you," he said, courteously.

"You must believe me," she cried with passion. "I beg of you to go. You have been here too long already," and a fire kindled in the eyes which the Gascons call lucky, the eyes of hazel and green, which made her husband lean forward and look long and searchingly into her face.

At last he said:

"You are still cherishing that madness of which you spoke, long since. Can you suppose that while you believe this thing of me, I will ever leave you? That would serve only to deepen your madness and increase your suffering. Do you not understand?"

"You are intricate," she cried. "You have the subtlety of the Evil One himself."

The man straightened, and rose from his chair. When he spoke, the quality of his voice had changed completely.

"I am sorry, Madame. There are others to be considered besides yourself. School yourself, Madame, to the inevitable."

He lifted her hand to his lips, and without another word turned and left her.

"Ah," exclaimed Bertrande bitterly, "that was the true manner of Martin Guerre. He has profited well from my complaints, this impostor."

Then began for the woman a long game of waiting and scrutinizing. Some day, she told herself, he will be off his guard, some day, if I do not warn him too often, I shall catch him in his deception, and free myself of him. "Ah, Martin, Martin," she cried in her loneliness, "where are you and why do you not return?" And as she observed the man whom she now called the impostor, considered the tranquillity of his demeanor and the ease with which he accomplished all his designs, confidently winning all people to him, the terrifying thought occurred to her that his great sense of security might lie in some certain knowledge, unshared by herself or by anyone else at Artigues. Perhaps the real Martin was indeed dead. Perhaps this man had seen his body on some distant battlefield, besmeared with blood and mutilated, the face turned downward to the bloody grass.

Perhaps, and at this last thought her soul recoiled in horror, perhaps he had himself slain Martin Guerre that he might come to Artigues in perfect safety and inherit his lands.

She watched him as he sat by the fire, fatigued from the day's work, yet playing gently with the children, holding the youngest child upon his knee, and discoursing meanwhile to Sanxi, and he did not appear a monster. The priest came still, through the winter evenings, as before Bertrande had made her momentous confession, and, hearing the talk between the curé and the master of the house, Bertrande could not but admit that this man was wise, subtle, and, if not learnèd, infinitely skilled in argument. The priest valued him, the children loved him, and these virtues of his which entrenched him with those who should have supported her, but made her the more bitter against him. Passionate as had once been her love for this stranger, so passionate became her hatred of him, and her fear; yet in order that his power over her might not become greater, she dissembled her hatred and veiled her fear; for this reason and also because the innocent and observant eyes of Sanxi were upon her. Now all the years of loneliness before the return of Martin Guerre, or rather, before the coming of the impostor, stood her in good stead. She enclosed in her heart a single fierce determination, and outwardly her life went on as usual.

Still, she sickened. When her pallor was mentioned to her, she explained it by her physical condition. She grew more thin in cheek and shoulder as her belly grew more round. The bones of her face, the delicate arch of the nose, the high cheek bones, the wide and well-shaped skull, defined themselves under the white skin, and beneath the high arching brows her lucky eyes shone with an extraordinary luminosity.

Her husband was extremely attentive to her health, ordering all things that he could imagine to increase her comfort, excusing her from work whenever it was possible, and if there was a battle between them, apparently only Bertrande herself was aware of it. Sometimes she wondered, so unfailing were his courtesies, whether he was indeed aware of the fact that they were enemies. However, in the beginning of the spring and toward the termination of her pregnancy, an incident occurred which defined their positions beyond any doubt.

Martin's younger sister and her husband, Uncle Pierre Guerre, the curé and Martin Guerre himself, whom Bertrande called the impostor, were returning from mass at Artigues to Martin's farm. As they approached the inn, the landlord, leaning from an upper story window—for the ground floor was given over to the accommodation of the horses of his guests, according to custom—called to Martin Guerre:

"Hollah, Master Guerre, here is a friend of yours from Rochefort, an old comrade in arms who asks the way to your house."

He drew in his head, turning around to speak to a person in the room behind him, and as Martin's party came up to the door of the inn, there issued from that door a thick-set figure wearing a coat of link armor over a red woolen jerkin, who carried a cross-bow slung over one shoulder and a short sword fastened to his belt. His face was scarred from more than battle wounds, and one eye was clouded by some kind of infection that was gradually masking the lens.

"I was at Luchon," he said, coming close to them, without hesitation, "soaking my old carcass and my scabby hide in that unspeakable mud. It smells of bad eggs, pah, but it is warm, and that feels good. There I learned of your being home again, and I came to stretch my legs before your fire. Eh, Martin, we shall have much to say of Picardy, eh, and other matters less heroic." He laughed, thrusting his thumbs through his belt, but the man whom he addressed neither laughed nor smiled but regarded him with a somewhat puzzled countenance.

"Eh, Martin?" repeated the soldier, and, indicating by a nod of his head Martin's younger sister, "Is this your wife?"

"My friend of Rochefort," said Martin slowly, "I cannot for the life of me remember when or where we met. I am not so certain that we ever met at all."

The soldier cocked his head to one side, and then, with the gesture of a man who feels the leg of a spavined horse, bent quickly, and grasping Martin below the left knee, gave the leg a sharp squeeze and then a slap. Straightening himself abruptly, he announced:

"Certainly, you do not remember me! You are not even sure you know me, eh? Impostor! You are Monsieur Martin Guerre, my friend? You return from the mass, you are neat and proper, you have a great distaste for the smelly old soldier! You are nothing but a fraud. The true Martin Guerre—I knew him very well. There was a man. He could see beyond the dirt on the face of a friend. He lost a leg before St. Quentin in the year fifty-seven."

There was a dead silence, during which Martin Guerre lifted his left eyebrow the while he contracted the right, a trick, as his sister remembered, which had been characteristic of his father.

Then Uncle Pierre said:

"Brute! You have the manners of a pig. Take yourself away before you force me to roll you in the dirt."

"I do not go away so easily," said the soldier from Rochefort. The man whom he had accused still regarded him calmly, and slowly remarked:

"Doubtless he wishes me to bribe him to leave. I have heard that there was employed under the Duke of Savoy a man who resembled me greatly in feature. Perhaps it was he who lost a leg."

"Ventre de Dieu," exclaimed the soldier with increased impatience and scorn. "I knew him well, the true Martin Guerre. He was a Gascon and he lost his left leg at the battle of St. Laurent before St. Quentin. It is all one to me if this man is a rogue. He is your relative, not mine. If he had been Martin Guerre, he would have known me."

And with many oaths he turned back to the inn, of which all the windows now stood wide open as those within tried to see and hear what went on; he was still cursing under his breath and in more languages than one as he disappeared within the shadow of the doorway, but he made no further effort to have his story believed.

"He is malicious," said Pierre Guerre with indignation, as the small party proceeded on the way to the farm.

"He was disappointed," said Martin. "He thought to find a welcome with good lodging and food for a week. I do not grudge him the food, but I cannot have him sitting about every evening telling stories of gallant adventures—which I did not commit—before my wife, who is so sick."

The curé said nothing, but Martin's sister and uncle discussed the matter of having the soldier apprehended.

"Let it pass," said Martin. "It was a mistake; there is truly a man who resembles me. I have heard of him more than once. And the fellow was disappointed. Had he been less foul with disease I would have brought him home with us anyway, to hear the news from Spain." To the priest he added, "I could wish that this had not happened."

The priest nodded, said nothing, but the sister continued indignant and voluble, and when they reached the farm, and found Bertrande waiting for them in the kitchen, she burst at once into an account of the adventure.

"Imagine it," exclaimed Uncle Pierre as the young woman paused for breath. "Only imagine it! He leaned over, this pig of a man, and pinched Martin below the knee as if he had been a horse for sale at the market. I wonder that he did not offer to look at his teeth."

"He called Martin a rogue," repeated the sister, ever more indignant. "Worse than that," said the brother-in-law. "He called Martin an impostor."

Bertrande, looking from one hot, excited face to another, turned at last her brilliant eyes full upon her husband's quiet countenance, in a look of triumph and scorn.

"At last," she cried suddenly in a strange hoarse voice, "at last, dear God, Thou wilt save me!"

She pressed her hands to her temples, then turned, and ran from the room.

"Go with her," said Martin, his face immediately full of concern. "Go with her quickly, my sister. Do you not see? She is ill." To the priest he said, "You understand to what a pass it has come? I would give half my farm if this soldier from Rochefort had never come to Luchon. This will unsettle her reason."

The sister, who had followed Bertrande, found her kneeling beside the bed, clutching the coverlet in agony. To all questions and reproaches she answered only:

"I am dying, I am dying. I beg of you, send for my nurse."

She was delivered that night in great suffering of a daughter who died before she had lived an hour. Bertrande herself was very ill, and in the fever which followed the birth of the child, asked only to see the soldier from Rochefort. To humor her, for he thought her hours were numbered, the curé sent for the soldier, but the man was not to be found. He had not lingered at Artigues. He had been seen at St. Gaudens some days later. After that all trace of him was lost. However, the curé caused to be written down and properly witnessed and signed the accounts of those who heard the soldier's accusation, and these papers he brought to the invalid. Immediately after she had received them, the condition of Madame Guerre began to improve, a fact which could not fail to impress not only the curé but her entire family

"She is mad," they said to each other, "but if we humor her and are patient, God willing, she may recover."

The improvement continued. She gained strength slowly but steadily and was soon able to walk about a little in her room, but she refused steadily to leave the Chamber. She refused likewise to see her husband, to admit him to her room, or in any way to have anything to do with him. Everyone on the farm could see how heavily this weighed upon the master. He was as patient as ever with his people, and as kind, but there was little merriment.

"Madame is not herself since her illness," the housekeeper said to the priest, "and it is breaking the Master's heart."

The priest sought out Martin Guerre, and found him at work in the fields. Together they sat down in the shade of the beech trees, and the priest said:

"Who would have thought that kindness could have worked so much sorrow!"

Martin shook his head.

"There would have been no sorrow, Father, if I had not tried to run away from my father's anger. The trouble begins there. But what shall I do to help her? Once she asked me to leave her."

The priest surveyed his friend intently. If this man were not indeed his friend and the son of his friend, surely his eyes would betray him.

"And you refused to leave?" the priest said.

"At that time I refused," said the man before him, evenly, his sad eyes meeting those of the priest without hesitation. "I thought that to leave her then would but confirm her in this madness, and that I should be deserting her to years of pain—as if I were to fasten upon her the guilt of a sin—" he hesitated—"a sin of which she must not be accused."

His voice was vehement, and he stopped speaking abruptly, overcome with emotion. To the priest, who knew the voice, who knew the face, there could be no doubt whatever but that the grief, the concern and the humility were real. He passed a hand over his forehead and looked away toward the empty wheat field.

"My son," he answered at last, "I do not know what to advise you. What you have said is true. If you run away—if you disappear again—it will look like an admission of guilt. Unless, of course, you go with my consent and knowledge, leaving word of where you may be found, and denying the accusation of the fellow from Rochefort. It is conceivable that your absence might improve the condition of your wife. Your presence but adds continual fuel to the fire. The spirit is ill, and it has need of rest to heal itself, of rest as well as prayer. But you cannot leave the farm indefinitely. Your people have need of you. The parish, also—I have need of you. Is there no journey you could make about some business of the farm?"

Martin shook his head.

"The business of the farm is all in the parish of Artigues."

"You left a sum of money with your uncle when you were a boy. I think that it has never been spent. Take it, and journey to Toulouse and there purchase a gift for Our Lady. Be home again before the snow. Say farewell to your wife before you go."

"She will not speak to me," said the man with a wry smile. "But I shall say farewell to you before I go. I must help them with the wheat harvest before I leave. Meanwhile"—he hesitated—"let us say nothing of the matter until it is accomplished. There will be less talk."

The priest nodded, and blessed him. Martin Guerre returned to his work.

A few days later Bertrande herself sent for Pierre Guerre. The honest man found her seated in the high-backed chair near the curtained bed, but as he approached her, she rose.

"I have sent for you, my uncle," she said in a low voice, "because you are still the head of our family, and I must beseech your help."

The room was cool, and to the diminished vitality of the invalid it seemed even cold. She stood wrapped in her black wool capuchon, the hood thrown back on her shoulders. Her illness had aged her, but there showed in her face such poise and clarity of spirit that the uncle was unaccountably moved.

"Sit down, my child," he said gently. "You will tire yourself."

She shook her head.

"I ask you to believe me, believe me at last, when I say to you now, 'I am not mad.' All my household believe me to be mad. I have only yourself to whom to look for help."

"I believe you, my child," he answered quietly. "Sit down. Look, I will sit down beside you on the coffer."

"I have no proof," said she, "unless the story of the soldier from Rochefort can be considered proof."

"It is a strange story," replied the uncle. "I was angered that day, but since then, the picture seems to move, like people changing places in a dance. If there is another man who resembles Martin, this must be the man. You are Martin's wife, and you would be the first to know. Moreover, he has behaved strangely of late."

"In what manner?" said Bertrande.

"He came to me demanding a sum of money which he left with me before he ran away. I replied that the money had made part of the sum for the purchase of the lower fields. It was a matter of which his father had approved. The purchase was made after his father's death, according to his father's plan."

"I remember," said Bertrande. "What then?"

"He was angered," said Pierre shortly.

"I understand," said Bertrande slowly. "He wishes money in hand in order to leave us. Now that he fears detection, now that he has pillaged us, now that he has almost killed me, he will go away." She began to weep and hid her face in her hands.

A deliberate, abiding wrath grew in the old uncle as he watched her bent head and listened to her sobs. "Madame," he said, striking with his clenched hand upon his knee, "give me your permission to accuse this man of his crime. He shall not leave us unpunished."

Bertrande could hardly speak for her tears. But:

"Accuse him, punish him, do as you like with him, only rid me of his presence," she implored.

Less than a week later armed men from Rieux arrived at the farm and arrested the master of the house. They brought him in irons from the field to the kitchen for a final identification by Bertrande. His own men followed after, angry and sullen. Standing beside the master's chair, before the hearth, Bertrande identified him as the man who had claimed, but falsely, to be her husband.

"I accuse him," she said clearly, "of being an impostor and not the true Martin Guerre."

It was the first time since the birth of the child that she had left her room. Uncle Pierre stood beside her. It was evident that the men from Rieux had been expected.

Sanxi, seeing his father in chains, burst into a passion of weeping, flung himself, first upon his father, and then, kicking and scratching, upon the two guardsmen.

"Madame," said his father quietly, above the turmoil thus raised, "is it indeed you who do this to me?"

Bertrande bowed her head, and turned her back upon him.

The man sighed, and nodded, as if to himself. Then, turning to the housekeeper, he asked that the youngest child be brought. The old woman, all in tears, held up the little one to his father to be kissed. The people of the farm crowded about, and the priest, entering in haste, cried to the men-at-arms:

"This is folly—you do not know what you are doing!" He stretched out his hands and would have prevented their departure.

"Let be," said the prisoner, still quietly. "It is not the fault of the men. They must do as they have been commanded." And then, addressing his people, he said: "Good-by, my children. God willing, I shall return to you safely."

"It is a mistake," said the priest again to the guardsmen. "You do not understand that the woman is mad."

But the guard moved forward, with the prisoner between them, through the wide doorway into the courtyard of the farm. The housekeeper, Sanxi and the other servants followed closely behind them. There was some delay in the courtyard as a horse was brought for the prisoner. Bertrande, who had continued to stand with her back to the room, her eyes upon the hearth, turned now and looked about her. She was entirely alone. In the courtyard the servants shouted their last farewells. She heard Sanxi's voice.

"Good-by, my father, my dear father!"

II. Rieux

The accusation had been made at Rieux, since Artigues was too small a place to boast a court, and thither Bertrande went with her uncle, Pierre, and the servants who were to be called as witnesses. She stayed in the house of her mother's sister, occupying the same room which she had been given on her earlier visit, and in which the sun had always seemed to shine through western windows in the morning. But this time the sun shone from the east, as it should do, and Bertrande marveled that she had ever felt confused about the direction. In the same fashion she marveled that she should have permitted herself to be deceived concerning the identity of the man who had called himself her husband. Her present belief was inescapable and plain, and yet she found herself alone in it, alone, that is, save for the support of honest Pierre. She left in Artigues a house in which the very servants looked at her askance. Of Martin's four sisters, two had not hesitated to declare that they thought her malicious. They said openly, so that the report returned to her:

"For years during Martin's absence she was sole mistress of the farm. Now she cannot bear to be put back into her proper place. She has a greed of authority, and of money. She was severe to us before we married, severe and miserly. This is all a plan to destroy Martin and possess the farm."

The other sisters, particularly the youngest, defended her. She had done no more in the management of the estate and of the family than their mother would have required her to do, and her strange fancy that Martin was not her husband had arisen from the grief of the long separation. They were sure that she was insane. The charity and the coldness were alike difficult for Bertrande; and at Rieux, even her aunt supported the claim of the impostor.

"My poor child," she said to Bertrande, "your years of suffering have told on your brain in a strange way. Why, I have known the boy all his life! Of course I shall testify in his favor, if I am asked, and when the courts have decided that he is really your husband, perhaps you will have some peace, although it's all a great pother to go through with in order to convince a wife of what she ought to know without help."

At the first session of the court the crime was formally charged to the prisoner of misrepresentation and theft. Bertrande then demanded through Pierre Guerre, and in fact only because of the uncle's insistence, that the prisoner be made to do penance publicly, that he pay a fine to the king, and that he pay to herself the sum of ten thousand livres. She was then asked to state her reasons for the accusation.

"My lords," she began, "there is the testimony of the soldier from Rochefort."

She was interrupted.

"We ask you for your testimony only," they reminded her.

She bent her head, and after a moment, told them just what she had told the priest. Upon being questioned further, she added:

"I also found it curious, upon remarking the prisoner at sword practice with my son, that Martin Guerre should fence so awkwardly; he was known to be distinguished in the art."

The prisoner smiled, and shrugged his shoulder slightly. A brief smile also flitted across the face of one of the judges, and Bertrande, seeing it, exclaimed:

"You may smile, my lord, and my testimony may seem innocent to you and of small importance, but I swear by God and all His holy angels that this man is not my husband. Of that I am certain, though I should die for it."

"Well, we shall inquire, Madame, we shall inquire," said the justice, and called for the accused to be examined.

The prisoner stepped forward with an easy manner, as if he stood before his own hearth. He explained that during his absence he had served the King of Spain, that he had traveled extensively both through Spain and France, and that he had not known until he came to Rieux, some three years earlier, that his parents were dead; that upon learning that he was head of the house, he had made all haste to return to his wife and child, and had endeavored in every way to make up for his past neglect. He furnished the names and addresses of people who could verify the story of his wanderings. He told of his return to Artigues, of how Pierre Guerre, his uncle, had been the first person in the village to recognize and welcome him, and averred that Pierre had been to him in all things friendly until he, Martin, had found reason to question Pierre about the disposition of a certain sum of money which he had left in the care of his uncle. Since that time, he said, his uncle had sought to destroy him. He even hinted in conclusion that an attempt had been made upon his life.

The judges then asked him a great number of questions regarding the history of his family, the date of his own wedding, the date of birth of Sanxi, to all of which he answered without hesitation.

"Madame," said the judges to Bertrande, "you have heard these answers. Are they correct?"

"They are all correct, my lords," said Bertrande, "but still the man is not my husband."

The judges conferred together and presently announced that the case would be dismissed for a short time while an examination should be made into the characters of the accusers. Bertrande, her face burning with shame at this implication, turned to Martin's uncle.

"This is because we have asked for money," she said bitterly. "All that I ask, all that I hope is to be rid of his presence."

Uncle Pierre shrugged his shoulders.

"You must not be unreasonable," he told her. "After all, there will be the expense of the trial."

However, the investigation determined that the characters of Bertrande and Pierre were above reproach, and the case was ordered to proceed. In the interval, word of the dispute had gone round the countryside, and a great number of persons had either presented themselves voluntarily or had been called by the court as witnesses. On the morning when the case reopened, the chambers of the judges were crowded with interested persons, of whom no fewer than one hundred and fifty were present in the quality of witnesses.

The examination of relatives began, followed by that of the farm servants, then of neighbors from Artigues. Without a dissenting voice they all declared that the man in fetters was no other than Martin Guerre himself. The priest, being called, declared that the man was Martin and gave an eloquent account of Bertrande's illness and her madness, as he had discussed it with her husband and herself.

The day was wearing to a close, and Bertrande, sadly, said to Pierre Guerre:

"Do not all these people begin to convince you that you may be mistaken?"

"I am not one to change my mind every five minutes," said honest Pierre. "I have thought him a rogue, and a rogue he remains."

The priest departed and a new witness was called.

"Your name?" said the judge.

"Jean Espagnol."

"And whence do you come?"

"From Tonges, my lord."

"Your occupation?"

"Soldier of fortune."

"Do you know the prisoner?"

"That I do, my lord."

"And by what name do you know him?"

"Arnaud du Tilh, my lord. Sometimes we call him Pansette."

A murmur ran over the room. People stretched themselves, and Bertrande shot a glance at the accused man, whose face, however, showed no guilt, no surprise and only a very natural interest in the proceeding.

"And how long have you known the prisoner?"

"Oh, from the cradle, my lord."

"Have you had any conversation with him of late?"

"My lord, he told me less than half a year ago that he was playing the part of one Martin Guerre, that he had met this said Guerre in the wars, and that this Guerre made over to him, for certain considerations, the whole of his estate and the permission to impersonate himself."

"Ah, it is a lie," cried the voice of Bertrande, passionately.

"Well said, Madame," added the prisoner.

"Silence," demanded the judge.

The witness spread his hands palm outwards with the expression of a man who has done his best for the cause of truth and justice, and, being dismissed, took his place again in the crowd.

From then on the case began to appear most dubious for the prisoner, for although it was rather a tall story that Martin Guerre would have made over all his possessions to a wandering rogue for whatever considerations, there were many witnesses examined who declared that the prisoner was in fact a Gascon by the name of Arnaud du Tilh. There were also among the witnesses called, some who were acquainted with both Martin Guerre and the rogue du Tilh. Of these, some said that the prisoner was Martin, some that he was Arnaud, and some declared themselves unable to decide between the two. The examination of witnesses ran on at such length that it was necessary to reconvene the court on the following day. Finally, when the last witness had given his testimony, the judges sent for Sanxi, and tried to find in his face some resemblance to the man who claimed to be his father. But since the boy so obviously resembled his father's sisters, who were said to resemble their mother, rather than their father, the countenance of Sanxi was of little aid to the judges.

The judges withdrew and debated the case at length. Bertrande, sitting clasping and unclasping her hands, overheard two of the spectators who were commenting freely on the case. Said one:

"They have proved nothing against the man, and the woman demands a great sum of money."

"If she denies him to be her husband," said the other, "why did she not deny it immediately? She lived with him for three years without complaining. Why does she quarrel with him now?"

"She has lost her pains, without a doubt," said the first.

"My God, my God," said Bertrande, bowing her head and clasping and unclasping her long hands in a passion of despair, "deliver me from sin."

The judges returned and prepared to speak:

"Whereas, out of one hundred and fifty witnesses called by this court of Rieux, forty have testified that the prisoner is Martin Guerre, sixty have refused to testify to his identity, and fifty have testified that he is none other than Arnaud du Tilh, and whereas the wife of Martin Guerre, whose opinion should bear more weight with us than that of any other living person, has testified that the prisoner is not her husband, we do affirm that the prisoner is in fact Arnaud du Tilh, commonly known as Pansette. And we do condemn the said Arnaud du Tilh to do public penance before the church of Artigues, and before the house of Martin Guerre, and to suffer death by decapitation before the house of Martin Guerre."

A gasp as of astonishment and pity swept the room, and Bertrande de Rols, rising from her seat, cried out in a clear, terrified voice:

"Not death! Not death! No, no, I have not demanded his death!"

She stood, grown very pale, confronting the judges with surprise and horror in her features; and then, putting out her hand gropingly, she half-turned toward Pierre Guerre, and fell unconscious into his arms.

The prisoner had started also at Bertrande's cry. In spite of the sentence just passed upon him, his eyes were clear, and his face bright, one would have said, with joy.

III. Toulouse

It is difficult to relate all that Bertrande de Rols suffered in the days which followed directly upon this decision. She returned to Artigues, to a house in which all peace and contentment had been destroyed. Nor was there anyone in Artigues, except Martin's uncle, who did not by word or gesture blame her for this destruction. Sanxi regarded her with frightened, incredulous eyes, or slipped from a room as she entered, like a small animal who has been beaten continuously and without having offended. Nor was the matter ended. If the sentence had been carried through without delay, Bertrande felt, she might have borne the horror with some courage and reached, afterwards, a certain peace of finality, and time might have justified her action; but the case had been appealed at once by Martin's sisters to the parliament of Toulouse, and the summer dragged forward through a long, heartbreaking uncertainty.

The wheat was harvested, but without exultation, and threshed, but without merriment. As in other years the water of the mountain stream was turned upon the stubble fields and ran in shining cascades across the parched and broken earth, but Bertrande de Rols did not walk out to see it, nor did it matter to her that the flowers sprang up after the passage of the water as if a carpet had suddenly been spread, a carpet of a thousand flowers and a thousand pleasant odors. During the last days of August word was brought to Artigues that the parliament of Toulouse had found the evidence inconclusive and had called the witnesses for a second trial.

The curé visited Bertrande.

"My daughter," he said, as persuasive and kindly as if she had not now for almost a year steadily refused his advice, "it is no more than my duty to entreat you to consider once more that which you have undertaken."

"Reverend Father," said Bertrande abruptly, "have you never once thought but that I might be right? Consider the soldier from Rochefort. Is it not possible that this man may indeed be Arnaud du Tilh? Is it not more than likely?"

"All things are possible with God," said the priest, "but I cannot think it likely that the man of whom we speak should be one and the same with a most notorious rogue." His voice softened and his eyes became very sad. "The man of whom we speak was one whom I had grown to value greatly. His ways, his thoughts, were kindly. There was no soul in my parish of Artigues who did not benefit in some way from his presence here."

"You valued him," said Bertrande quietly, "more than you valued Martin Guerre who ran away?"

"Indeed, more," said the priest. "What was that boy? A raw, impatient youth, a thoughtless boy, selfish in the extreme. He had in him, it is true, the qualities of a great man. I like to think that he has grown into that man. His selfishness has become generosity, his impatience has become energy well-directed. It did not happen suddenly. He was eight years in a hard school." He paused, and in a curious voice asked her, "It does not pain you to hear me praise him?"

"No," she answered slowly, as if she questioned herself. "It is no more than just to remember that he has been kind to us—kind to all, save me, and kind even to me after a strange fashion."

"Then if it does not pain you to hear him praised," said the priest, pursuing his slight advantage, "if it pleases you a little to hear good of him, then you cannot have ceased entirely to love him, and does not this love convince you that he is truly Martin Guerre?"

"No," said Bertrande fiercely and quickly. "No, Father. Can you not see, it is in this love that he has wronged me most, that he has damned my soul? I have sinned, through him, and you will not understand it even long enough to give me absolution! No, Father, I cannot believe him to be other than the rogue, Arnaud du Tilh."

Her cheeks had flushed, as if with a fever, and to the priest her eyes held a strange luminosity. He lifted his hand and then, helplessly, dropped it upon his knee. He said:

"There is a doubt, nevertheless. While there remains a doubt you run the risk of unwillingly, unwittingly, assisting at the destruction of your own husband. I counsel you to withdraw the charges before it is too late. Those who love you, and him, have given you an opportunity of retreating from this whole affair.

"Is it for you to assume vengeance? You believe that you have sinned. You are in danger of sinning far more greatly. If there is evil in the matter, God will unravel it in His own good time. No, do not answer now. I advise you to withdraw the accusation. If you cannot do this, if your heart will not permit you to do this, then I shall pray for you that you may be prevented against your will from so harming, not only yourself, but all who love you."

He left her sorely shaken, as he had meant to do, not in her opinion of the man's guilt, but in her belief in the wisdom of her action. The event had gone beyond her plan. "I did not demand his death," she reminded herself; "but now I must demand it."

After the priest came Martin's youngest sister. She knelt in front of Bertrande and, covering Bertrande's two hands with her own, looked up into the face of her sister-in-law, and said most pleadingly:

"Bertrande, my dearest sister, we were always good friends. Do not be angry with me now. When you come before the judges of Toulouse, say to them, 'I withdraw the charges made against my husband. I do not know how it happened—I think that I was mad.' Our uncle will not press the charges, if you do not. Martin will forgive you. We shall all be happy again. Dear God," and she suddenly began to weep, "we cannot have him killed before his own house."

She bowed her head on her hands, and Bertrande felt upon her own cold fingers the warm tears.

"Little sister," she answered in despair, "how can I deny the truth?"

"It is only the truth for you, not for us," returned the weeping girl. "For the truth, that none of us believe, you would destroy us all. We shall never be happy again. The farm will never prosper again."

"Your uncle believes as I do," said Bertrande.

"Ah, but he is old. He wants nothing to be changed that was not just as it was when our father died. He would not change a cobble stone. And Martin changes everything, and is changed himself, so that we all love him more."

"Well, then," said Bertrande, "if the man be Martin, as you would have me say, why does not Arnaud du Tilh come forward and declare himself? Why should he let an innocent man suffer in his name?"

"He has enough to answer for with the law," replied the girl with some impatience. "It is to his advantage to be considered dead. The law will cease to seek for him. And why should a rogue put his neck into a halter for the sake of another?"

Bertrande sighed and laid her hand gently on the girl's shoulder.

"I am so sorry," she said, "so sorry." But she promised nothing.

September came, reddening the vines, making the mornings and evenings cool. Bertrande, returning from church the evening before her departure, whither she had gone in preparation for the journey to Toulouse, crossed the courtyard toward her house, wearily. She saw the housekeeper sitting near the doorway killing doves, and sat down beside the old woman.

"You have made your prayers, Madame," said the old woman.

"Yes."

"I wish that you had made them for a better cause."

"How can you know what prayers I made?"

"I cannot know, Madame. I only know that since you have had this strange idea of yours, nothing goes well for us. And all was well before. So well."

She sighed, leaning forward, holding the dove head down between her hands, the smooth wings folded close to the smooth soft body, while the dark blood dripped slowly from a cut in the throat into an earthen dish. The dish, already filled with blood, darker than that which was falling into it, spilled over slightly, and a barred gray cat, creeping cautiously near, elongated, its belly close to the ground, put out a rasping pale tongue and licked the blood. The housekeeper, after a little, pushed it away with the side of her foot. A pile of soft gray-feathered bodies already lay beside her on the bench. The living dove turned its head this way and that, struggled a little, clasping a pale cold claw over the hand that held it, and relaxed, although still turning its head. The blood seemed to be clotting too soon, the wound was shrunken, and the old woman enlarged it with the point of the knife which she had in her lap. The dove made no cry. Bertrande watched with pity and comprehension the dying bird, feeling the blood drop by drop leave the weakening body, feeling her own strength drop slowly away like the blood of the dove.

"What would you have me do?" she asked at length. "The truth is only the truth. I cannot change it, if I would."

The old woman turned her head without lifting her shoulders, still leaning forward heavily above her square, heavy lap. Her face was much more lined than in the days when Bertrande had first known her. There were creases above and below her lips, parallel with the line of the lips, as well as creases at the corners of the mouth. Her forehead was scored with lines that arched one above the other regularly, following the arches of the eyebrows. There were fine radiating lines about her eyes. The skin was brown and healthy, with ruddy patches on the cheek bones, but nevertheless the face was worn.

"I, Madame?" she said.

Bertrande looked into the tired affectionate brown eyes and nodded.

"Ah," said the housekeeper, turning once more to the dove which now lay still in her hands, "Madame, I would have you still be deceived. We were all happy then." She laid the dead dove with the others, and stooped to pick up the dish of blood.

All the way to Toulouse the echoes of these three conversations rang through the mind of Bertrande de Rols, making a slow, confused accompaniment to the clop-clop of the horses' hooves. The housekeeper rode behind her, Uncle Pierre before. They descended the valley of the Neste, the road running close to the stream, until the valley closed about them narrowly, leaving barely room for the passage of the torrent and the path above it. The woods were yellowing, but were still rich in leafy shadow. They came from the deep gorge to the wider valley of the Garonne, the stream coming in swiftly from the right, from the valley of Aran, saw St. Bertrand de Comminges with its narrow buttresses rising from its stony pedestal far below them in the green cup of the hills, crossed the Garonne and came into the more spacious country where the heavy-laden vines were trained from maple tree to maple tree in natural festoons. They passed St. Gaudens and St. Martory; they approached Muret. It was the journey which Bertrande had taken in imagination with Martin that autumn when he had first left her, and it was all rich and lovely, the wild mountain scenery giving way gradually to more thickly clustered farms, thorn hedges around the autumn gardens, and fruit trees set about the houses, medlars, plums and cherries, and always the fresh running of the water beyond the road; but now she traveled in great bitterness of heart, hearing through the noise of the hooves and the splashing of the Garonne, only the reproaches and prayers of those dependent upon her.

It had come to be a fixed idea with her that Martin was dead. It was incredible to her that any man could stand so calmly to face the extravagant charges brought against him as Arnaud du Tilh had done, if he had not certain knowledge that the man was dead whose place he usurped. Justly or unjustly she believed also that du Tilh had had something to do with Martin's death. Being so bereaved, and so unjustly blamed, herself, she would have welcomed almost any plan that would have given her back the sympathy and understanding of those she loved. And they had entreated her to withdraw the charges against du Tilh. Well, and if she did? Was it too late? Might she not restore to them the happier days?

"I, Madame? I could wish you still to be deceived."

The words recurred to her again and again. Might she not purchase for her people with this one secret weight of shame against her soul the peace and happiness which she desired for them, and for herself their forgiveness and gratitude?

Again, if the court of Toulouse should reverse the decision of the court of Rieux, what then? Might she not feel released from this necessity of pursuit and revenge? The judges of Toulouse were very learnèd men and very near to the king in authority. The king, in turn, was appointed of God. Might she not consider it in some sense an indication from heaven, if the court should command her to receive this man as her husband, and might she not thereby find peace?

She had not seen the man whom she accused since the day in court when she had cried out against the sentence of death. His face had grown a little shadowy, the whole quality of his person a little unreal. Riding in the late afternoon under the shadow of trees, and out from that shadow into the light of a meadow, then again into the shadow of other, farther trees, she let herself slip for a time into a dream of surrender, and drooping over the saddle-bow, giving herself easily to the slow motion of the horse, she thought only of the restored tranquillity in the big kitchen, the contented faces bent above the evening meal—little of the man seated in the chair by the hearth, and, for the time being, nothing of herself in that new and impossible relationship. Meanwhile Pierre Guerre rode before her, and when she lifted her eyes from the roadway, or from the contemplation of the roadside grass, she saw his broad and honest back going steadily on.

She remembered then that he was not only her one supporter in the task which she had undertaken, but that he was also the one remaining defender of the old authority of her husband's house. He was that authority, simple and direct, without need of subterfuge or of superfluous charm, which before the coming of the stranger had kept them all in a secure and wholesome peace. He was for her that day a tradition more potent than the church. In her country the church had sometimes been denied, but even the Albigenses, hunted from town to town, from town to mountain cavern, and mercilessly destroyed for that denial, had never denied the tradition of which Pierre Guerre was the symbol. When she lay down that night in a strange bed in a strange valley, it was with a fatigue which overwhelmed body and soul, so that she felt she would have been fortunate never to waken.

On the third day of their journey they had come to the lowlands, and the September heat was excessive. There were no more cool ravines with belated shadows, where the water dripped from rocks, and where ferns grew. Now the fields lay parched and dusty. A white dust rose constantly from the road under the horses' hooves, and the leaves of the plane trees were dulled by dust. Earlier in the day they traversed the waste lands, filled with rocks and patches of wild lavender. At noon the heat was so great that they stopped to rest for nearly three hours under a grove of plane trees. Here there was shade for them and for their beasts, but the cicadas, boring into the bark of the trees for cooling drinks in the hot weather, beat their cymbals so loud in their great content, at the heat, at the sweet liquid which they sucked all day, that the whole grove rang, harshly reverberant. The air seemed to tremble to the sound, and for Bertrande they were a torment made audible. She was glad to resume the way, although the noise of the cicadas accompanied them still, now near, now far, as they passed other groves.

The Garonne ran, broader now, no longer splashing and sparkling, but sullenly, a yellow flood weighted with earth from the mountain-sides where the goats browsed. They crossed it toward evening over a wooden bridge into the city of Toulouse. Farther downstream, the first four arches of the Pont Neuf, the new stone bridge which was to be so well and so cleverly constructed that it would withstand even the most violent of the spring floods, projected its incompleted ramp less than half way across the yellow tide. Before them on the quay, the western sunlight shone full upon the whitened brick façade of Notre Dame de la Dalbade, and behind them the Pyrenees, of which a long spur had accompanied them almost to the city, retreated range upon snowy range, now turning slowly rose-color, far away, even into Spain. Behind La Dalbade lay Toulouse, a huddle of buildings of a dusty, rose-colored brick, intricate, noisy and odorous. The mountain peasants crossed the quay, passed the white façade of the church, and plunged into the network of echoing streets.

They found an inn and ordered supper, after engaging lodging for the night. The ordinary was full of guests, mostly merchants from the neighboring small towns, with a sprinkling of city men. Bertrande found a place in a corner, and, leaning back against the stained plastered wall, took refuge from herself and her companions in the public confusion of the room. Gradually, through the fog of personal misery which enveloped her, she observed that the talk was not general and easy, as one might have expected it to be, but that a group of men was giving great attention to a small number of travelers, and that there was a great deal of head-shaking, and of sober looks. When the hostess brought her supper, she detained her long enough to ask of what the men were talking.

"Of Amboise, Madame. You have heard nothing of Amboise?"

Bertrande shook her head.

"You are Catholic, Madame?"

Bertrande nodded.

"And so am I, Madame, but Amboise was the work of the Guises. God be praised, we have no such Catholics in Toulouse. It seems there was a conspiracy of a sort, not greatly proved—there was more talk than evidence. And for that—every kind of death: hangings, decapitations, drownings, without number every day, and so for a whole month. I am Catholic like yourself, Madame, but in Toulouse for every Catholic there is at least one Protestant. And they are good people, Madame. I promise you, I would as soon cut off my own head as that of my neighbor, and that for his being merely a Protestant!"

"But judging from those faces," said Pierre Guerre, indicating the talkers on the other side of the room, "one would think it a rebellion sooner than a conversation."

"A rebellion, yes," said the hostess. "I would not think it impossible. Toulouse has not always been bound to the French crown."

She went off, and the somber discussion continued, never more animated, never less intense, like a storm cloud that hangs patiently at the edge of an horizon, waiting for a wind to blow it into action.

"I do not know what is the matter with the world," said Pierre Guerre. "It seems to be breaking up in little pieces. In the days of Francis we were strongly French."

The room in which they slept, the entire party of mountaineers, for the inn was crowded, was hot and close. In the morning the streets were still warm and in the unmoving air the odors and stenches of the previous days remained, like a kind of disembodied refuse. There was none of the early morning crispness of the mountains, nor the amplitude of the purified air in which odors of the farm, of the beasts and of cooking, stood like symbols of the force and vigor, the healthiness of life. Bertrande awoke unrefreshed and felt in the air, as in her mind, the sultriness which paralleled the sullen temper of the men in the eating-room the evening before.

After the cup of wine, which seemed sour, and a piece of bread, which seemed bitter, she followed Pierre Guerre bare-headed through the streets to the council chambers of the Parliament in the Château Narbonnais.

The streets were crowded. People were speaking, not the mountain patois, but Languedocien, and with a curiously clanging, hard resonance, which made, in the narrower passages, everything seem to be spoken twice, re-echoed in metallic vigor from the dusty walls. And all the way Bertrande asked of herself, What am I doing here, in this unhappy town, in this prolonged stench, this heat, this desolating strangeness? I am pursuing a man to his death, a man who has been many times kind to me, who is the father of my smallest child. I am destroying the happiness of my family. And why? For the sake of a truth, to free myself from a deceit which was consuming me and killing me. She remembered herself speaking to Martin's sister.

"What would you have, my sister? The truth is only the truth. I cannot change it."

The sister had replied:

"It is true only for you."

"And might I be wrong?" she asked herself again as she mounted the stone steps and stood waiting before the great, closed door. She felt, in approaching this tribunal of Toulouse, a finality she had not felt at Rieux. It would not be possible for her to appeal this decision. It waited for her, behind those doors, in the quality of a doom. Suddenly her confidence deserted her, and terror engulfed her. She saw herself as borne forward helplessly on a great tide of misunderstanding and mischance to commit even a greater sin than that of which she had been afraid. The words of the priest returned to her. It had been holy counsel; she had refused it. She broke into a heavy sweat which turned cold on her skin and made her shudder even in the meridional heat. She was dizzied. The door before her grew insubstantial, invisible, as if she had walked into an icy cloud on the summit of La Bancanère. Blindly, she reached out her hand for Uncle Pierre, and, the doors being opened, she entered the courtroom leaning on his arm.

The judges of Toulouse wished to confront the two accusers with the accused, but singly, feeling that much might be revealed to the acute observer in the countenances of the accusers which had not been recorded in the account of the case forwarded to them by the judges of Rieux. Accordingly, once inside the courtroom, Bertrande was constrained to leave the support of Uncle Pierre, and, attended by a guard, advanced before the very seat of the judges. A hum of voices which had filled the room ceased suddenly as she appeared. In the abrupt silence she heard the admonition and then the question of the judge and, lifting her eyes, saw before her at the distance of only a few feet, the man for whom she had felt for one extraordinary year a great and joyous passion. He was regarding her with a look at once patient, tender and ironic. In her distress she saw no other face, and could not bear the contemplation of that tender gaze. She looked down, dropping her head forward, while the blood beat upward into her face and then receded. Who was this Arnaud du Tilh? What manner of man was he that he did not return her hatred with hatred, and why had he not made good his escape from this most dangerous justice on the day when she had first suspected him? Her face turned very white, while a return of the giddiness which had seized her just before she entered the court made it almost impossible for her to continue standing. She replied to the questions of the judges in a half-audible voice, and was then escorted to a small doorway through which she gained the courtyard, the sunlight, and a degree of solitude. She was instructed to return to the inn and to remain there until sent for. She went to her room and lay down.

Inside of an hour Pierre Guerre, who had been similarly instructed, joined her there. He was morose, annoyed at being detained at the inn, feeling himself a prisoner and having no occupation, large or small, with which to while away the time. He felt that he had behaved badly at the trial, and it was true that, although his conviction was as sound as ever, his manner had been hesitating, and embarrassed. He had felt himself stared at and smiled at as a peasant, a mountaineer. He had overheard, as the guard led him through the crowded room, an amused comment on his dress, the wit of which he had not understood, but the intent of which he had understood only too well. Annoyed at the crowd, humble before the judges, suddenly for the first time in his life acutely self-conscious, he had lost, for the space of five minutes, the simple dignity which had lent, at Rieux, such great weight to his testimony. Added to this discomfort was the spectacle of the impostor who had lost during his period of imprisonment some of his healthy brown color but none of his air of being arrogantly in the right.

"We are lost," said old Pierre to himself as he returned to the inn. "If it depended on me, we are lost indeed."

He dared not mention his discomfort to his niece, but it was the principal reason for the morose silence with which he rejoined her and set himself to wait out the day.

Bertrande lay upon the bed and regarded the stained canopy. Or she turned her head idly and surveyed the wall, or the figure of old Pierre seated on a straight bench under the window. She felt a great illness. A weight seemed to lie upon her breast which made breathing difficult, and the air which entered her lungs, after she had made so great an effort to expand them, contained no freshness, no reviving quality. Her mind had gone numb through prolonged self-examination. Exhausted and trapped by all these walls, by all these circumstances, she lay still and remembered that the one thing she desired was to be free of Arnaud du Tilh.

Meanwhile the court was proceeding with the examination of witnesses. One hundred and fifty witnesses had been called from the hearing at Rieux, and thirty new ones. Jean

Espagnol testified as he had done at the former trial, and introduced a friend, Pelegrin de Liberos by name.

Pelegrin de Liberos, being sworn, testified that he was an old friend of Arnaud du Tilh, and that Arnaud had recently not only admitted his identity to him, but had given him a handkerchief to be delivered to Arnaud's brother, Jean du Tilh.

Gradually a body of information was built up, minute details contributed now by one witness, now by another. The shoemaker of Artigues testified that the foot of Martin Guerre exceeded slightly that of the accused. Certain witnesses to the number of five who had formerly testified with assurance that the accused was indeed Martin Guerre, now declared that they could not be sure whether he was or whether he was not. Of the thirty new witnesses, twelve declared themselves unable to make any decision regarding the identity of the accused. He might be either Martin Guerre or Arnaud du Tilh, for all they could observe. On the other hand, seven of the new witnesses were quite sure that he was du Tilh, and ten were equally convinced that he was Martin Guerre. It was established that Martin Guerre had appeared to be taller and more slender than Arnaud du Tilh, and that he had been somewhat round-shouldered. However there was also the argument that since the accused was eleven years older than was Martin Guerre when last seen, the natural increase in weight and age might make him seem shorter than had appeared Martin Guerre, the boy of twenty.

Still, as the day went on, it was decided beyond a doubt that Martin Guerre had two teeth broken in the lower left jaw, as had also the accused; that Martin Guerre had a scar on the right eyebrow and the trace of an ulcer on one cheek, as had also the accused; that Martin Guerre had a drop of extravasated blood in the left eye, as had also the prisoner; that Martin Guerre had the nail of the left forefinger missing, and three warts on the left hand, two of which were on the little finger, as had also the man in fetters. So that the evidence tended well toward the defense, when there appeared before the judges an old man in the clothes of a mountaineer but with a somewhat more distinguished bearing than the costume might have seemed to warrant. He was sworn and his name was asked.

"I am called Carbon Bareau."

"And do you recognize the prisoner?"

"Gentlemen, this man in irons is the child of my own sister."

The old man then began to weep, and it was some time before he had recovered composure sufficient to continue.

"I have loved this boy," he said at last, "for he has a way with him, a way of stealing the heart, but I have feared for him ever since he grew old enough to talk. He has had no respect for the laws, gentlemen. It breaks my heart to say that he has even declared there is no God. He has revered his parents not at all. With no faith, no respect for family, nor for the law of the kingdom, what could one hope for, gentlemen? He has a good heart, that is all. But what is a good heart when he can so disgrace an honorable family?"

The two brothers of Arnaud du Tilh were then called and testified that the prisoner "resembled" their brother. Further than that they would not commit themselves.

After this came a long succession of witnesses for the defense, forty–five people all of blameless reputation and well-qualified to know what they were talking about. Martin's four sisters testified that the accused was their brother, as did also two brothers-in-law. Many people who had been guests at the wedding of Bertrande and Martin testified that the accused was certainly Martin Guerre. The curé of Artigues testified in favor of his friend.

Last witness of all came the old housekeeper who had brought to the bridal couple the little midnight repast, or réveillon. She had a story to tell after she had identified the prisoner as her young master. She stood before the judges with her hands clasped firmly at her belt, her brown eyes, good, honest, kind, fixed steadily upon the revered faces, and cleared her throat. Shortly after the return of Monsieur, she testified, she had heard Madame remark to Monsieur that she had kept certain chests unopened since his departure, so long ago. Upon hearing this, Monsieur had described certain white culottes wrapped in a piece of taffeta and requested that they be fetched him. Whereupon Madame had given to the housekeeper the key to the chest and requested her to fetch the *pantalons*, and the housekeeper had done so, finding them wrapped exactly as Monsieur had described. She made her recital bravely, greatly impressed herself at the gravity with which the judges heard it, and then, trembling with triumph and embarrassment, crept back to her place.

It was now late in the afternoon. The day's heat seemed to have accumulated in the crowded room along with the testimony of the witnesses, and the place was stifling. The light which entered through the high windows struck almost levelly upon the wall opposite, above the heads of the judges. The scribe laid down his pen, and the judges leaned forward to confer with each other. The examination was over, and it remained only to interpret the information. Those who had most to lose or gain by the decision had been dismissed to an inner room, but the courtroom was still packed.

It was neither reasonable nor just, the court argued first of all, to permit the bad reputation of the rogue Arnaud du Tilh to affect the fate of the prisoner if he was indeed Martin Guerre. Secondly, the judges argued, if it were so easy for the wife of Martin Guerre to mistake Arnaud for her husband, even if only for a short time, it would have been just as easy for the soldier from Rochefort to mistake Arnaud for Martin; there was no way of proving that the man who lost a leg at the battle of St. Laurent before St. Quentin was Martin Guerre rather than Arnaud du Tilh. Thirdly, they argued, it was beyond human ingenuity for any man to impersonate so well, to know so many intimate details of the life of another man, and to exhibit so close a physical resemblance to another man as the accused. Last of all, the court considered that the confusion of Bertrande at the sight of the accused, together with the report of her outcry in the court of Rieux when the sentence of death had been pronounced against the prisoner, testified badly for her case. Therefore the judges decided, and doubtless to their own relief, for they had been sadly puzzled, that the prisoner must be in truth none other than Martin Guerre, as he himself affirmed. The populace seemed pleased with the decision, and the clerk of the court prepared to put the verdict down in writing.

As this individual drew up his inkpot and sharpened his pen, and as the judges of Toulouse relaxed in their chairs and mopped their foreheads, conversing among themselves, and not, shrewdly, overlooking the smiles which overspread the courtroom, a commotion was heard at the outer door in which could be distinguished a great deal of stamping and of beating on the stone floor with the butt of a halberd, and a vigorous exposition of an undeterminable nature in an unmistakably

Gascon voice. The court sent to inquire; the messenger returned with news of some importance, for, as the audience twisted about and necks were craned in curiosity, a way was cleared through the crowd so that a Gascon soldier in travel-stained garments was permitted to walk directly up to the seats of the justices.

The halberds of the attendants sounded on the floor as the men halted, one on each side of the soldier; but there also sounded, during the entrance of the group, what resembled the butt of a third halberd, but which was, remarkably enough, a wooden leg worn by the Gascon soldier.

The judges surveyed the newcomer. He was sunburned, and bearded, but through the beard the shape of the high, cleft chin was easily discernible. His left eyebrow was scarred; and there was a trace of an old ulcer on one cheek. He returned the scrutiny of the judges of Toulouse with eyes which were arrogant, gray and cold.

"Body of God," said one of the justices, sinking back in his seat in something not unlike despair, "this is either Martin Guerre or the devil," and he gave an order to the attendants to put the newcomer under arrest.

After brief deliberation among the judges, the order was also given to remove the accused man to an adjoining chamber and to close the doors against further entrance. This done, the weary justices proceeded to examine the soldier with the wooden leg.

"I am without any doubt Martin Guerre," said the soldier. "I lost my leg before St. Quentin in the year fifty-seven. I am the father of Sanxi Guerre, and of no other children."

To all the questions which had previously been put to the accused man, the soldier was able to reply with reasonable accuracy. Once or twice his answers were at variance with those of Bertrande to the same question, now and again he hesitated before answering, but in the main he showed a knowledge of the affairs of Martin Guerre which might well have justified his claim to be that man. He also manifested an unusual knowledge of the career of Arnaud du Tilh. This was interesting, for the accused man had known nothing at all of the affairs of du Tilh; he had heard rumors of his existence — that was all. But the newcomer seemed no better informed concerning the affairs of Martin Guerre than the accused had seemed. At the end of an hour the judges were no nearer a decision than they had been early that morning.

There remained a final test, however. The prisoner was summoned and made to stand face to face with the one-legged soldier. Then, one by one, the relatives of the two men were called, and asked to make their choice.

Carbon Bareau, the first of the relatives of du Tilh to be called, stared for a moment with great surprise at the soldier, then, turning without any hesitation at all, laid his hand on the shoulder of the prisoner and said:

"Gentlemen, this is my nephew."

The brothers of Arnaud, confronted by the two men so extraordinarily similar, hesitated, and then, turning from the prisoner as from the soldier, besought the court to excuse them from bearing witness. The court, with a humanity rare in that century, dismissed them. They had in their request testified more than they realized.

When the youngest sister of Martin Guerre was admitted, she lifted her hands to her forehead in a gesture full of amazement and distress, and then, without hesitation, flung herself upon the breast of the soldier with the wooden leg and burst into tears. One by one the other relatives of Martin Guerre, being admitted, stared with surprise from the soldier to the prisoner and back again, and confessed with many apologies and protestations of sorrow at their mistake that the soldier with one leg was undeniably Martin Guerre, who had been so long away.

It was remarkable that while Martin Guerre received this succession of tearful recognitions with a consistent, stern reserve, Arnaud du Tilh the prisoner, although growing perceptibly graver, lost none of his calm air of assurance and none of his dignity.

Meanwhile the judges, seeing which way the case had turned, sent to their hotel for Pierre Guerre and Bertrande de Rols. The day had been long. For these two lonely defenders of a cause it had seemed longer than a century. When the messenger came for them, they left the confinement of the inn and followed him through the still-confining streets with the intense fatalism of the defeated. The messenger had been instructed to tell them nothing, but rumor had preceded the messenger with the advice that the case had been decided against them. Pierre Guerre was admitted alone, and Bertrande, left in an ante-chamber with a guard, was clearly and sharply aware for the first time in that exhausting day of one thing, and that was that she could not return to Artigues as the wife of Arnaud du Tilh.

After a time the door to the courtroom opened, and she was admitted. She made her way through the crowd toward the space before the judges. Without looking up to see it, she yet felt the intense curiosity of all these unfamiliar faces bent upon her like a physical force. In the silence of the room the insatiable interest of the crowd beat upon her like a sultry wave. She reached the open space, and stopped. There she lifted her eyes at last and saw, standing beside Arnaud du Tilh the man whom she had loved and mourned as dead. She uttered a great cry and turned very pale. The pupils of her parti-colored eyes, the lucky eyes, expanded until the iris was almost lost. Then, reaching out her hands to Martin Guerre, she sank slowly to her knees before him. He did not make any motion toward her, so that, after a little time, she clasped her hands together and drew them toward her breast, and, recovering herself somewhat, said in a low voice:

"My dear lord and husband, at last you are returned. Pity me and forgive me, for my sin was occasioned only by my great desire for your presence, and surely, from the hour wherein I knew I was deceived, I have labored with all the strength of my soul to rid myself of the destroyer of my honor and my peace."

The tears began to run quietly down her face.

Martin Guerre did not reply immediately, and in the pause which followed, one of the justices, leaning forward, said to Bertrande:

"Madame, we have all been very happily delivered from a great error. Pray accept the profound apologies of this court which did not earlier sufficiently credit your story and your grief."

But Martin Guerre, when the justice had finished speaking, said to his wife with perfect coldness:

"Dry your tears, Madame. They cannot, and they ought not, move my pity. The example of my sisters and my uncle can be no excuse for you, Madame, who knew me better than any living soul. The error into which you plunged could only have been caused by willful blindness. You, and you only, Madame, are answerable for the dishonor which has befallen me."

Bertrande did not protest. Rising to her feet, she gazed steadily into the face of her husband and seemed there to see the countenance of the old Monsieur, the patriarch whose authority had been absolute over her youth and over that of the boy who had been her young husband. She recoiled from him a step or two in unconscious self-defense, and the movement brought her near to the author of her misfortunes, the actual Arnaud du Tilh.

In the silence which filled the courtroom at Martin's unexpected severity, a familiar voice close to her elbow pronounced gently:

"Madame, you wondered at the change which time and experience had worked in Martin Guerre, who from such sternness as this became the most indulgent of husbands. Can you not marvel now that the rogue, Arnaud du Tilh, for your beauty and grace, became for three long years an honest man?"

"Sirrah," answered Bertrande, "I marvel that you should speak to me, whose devotion has deprived me even of the pity of my husband. I once seemed to love you, it is true. I cannot now hate you sufficiently."

"I had thought to ask you to intercede for mercy for me," said Arnaud du Tilh.

"You had no mercy upon me, either upon body or upon soul," replied Bertrande.

"Then, Madame," said du Tilh, and there was at last neither arrogance nor levity in his voice, "I can but die by way of atonement."

Bertrande had turned to look at him as he spoke. She turned now from him towards her husband, and then, without speaking, moved slowly toward the door. The court did not detain her, and the crowd, in some awe, drew aside enough to let her pass without interruption. Bertrande did not see the crowd. Leaving the love which she had rejected because it was forbidden, and the love which had rejected her, she walked through a great emptiness to the door, and so on into the streets of Toulouse, knowing that the return of Martin Guerre would in no measure compensate for the death of Arnaud, but knowing herself at last free, in her bitter, solitary justice, of both passions and of both men.

Arnaud du Tilh, being confined in the prison at Artigues in the days which followed immediately upon the hearing at Toulouse, made a confession in which he stated that he had been tempted to the imposture by the frequency with which he had been mistaken for Martin Guerre. All that he knew of Martin's life and habits he had gleaned from Martin's friends, from his servants and from members of his family. He added that he had not originally intended to take Martin's place in his household, but had intended to stay only long enough to pick up a little silver or gold.

The court decreed that he had been convicted of the several crimes of imposture, falsehood, substitution of name and person, adultery, rape, sacrilege, plagiat, which is the detention of a person who properly belongs to another, and of larceny; and the court condemned him to do penance before the church of Artigues on his knees, in his shirt, with head and feet bare, a halter around his neck and a burning taper in his hand, asking pardon of God and of the king, of Martin Guerre and of Bertrande de Rols, his wife; the court then condemned him to be handed over to the common executioner, who should conduct him by the most public ways to the house of Martin Guerre, in front of which, upon a scaffold previously prepared, he should be hanged and his body burned. All his effects were forfeit to the crown. And this decree bears the date of September the twelfth, in the year 1560, in the city of Toulouse.

Of Martin Guerre nothing more is recorded, whether he returned to the wars or remained in Artigues, nor is there further record of Bertrande de Rols, his wife. But when hate and love have together exhausted the soul, the body seldom endures for long.

The Return of Janet Lewis

Larry McMurtry

(From *The New York Review of Books*, June 11, 1998)

1.

In 1922 the printer-typographer Monroe Wheeler, who would go on to have a long and distinguished career with MoMA, set off to be a young-man-about-Europe. He was determined to publish poetry and publish it elegantly, to which end he established (first in Germany) an imprint called Manikin, under which he issued three booklets of verse. The first, *The Indians in the Woods*, was by a young Midwestern poet named Janet Lewis; William Carlos Williams's Go Go was the second; the third and last was *Marriage*, by Marianne Moore.

Not long before he left Illinois, Wheeler had got his feet wet typographically, so to speak, by publishing two books of verse now not easily secured: *The Bitterns*, by his friend Glenway Westcott, and *The Immobile Wind*, by a young teacher of languages named Arthur Yvor Winters, who had, not long before, been released from the Sunmount Sanatorium in Santa Fe, where he recovered from a serious bout with tuberculosis. Young Winters was soon to go off to Moscow, Idaho, to take the only teaching job he could get, but, on a trip to Chicago, he met Janet Lewis. Monroe Wheeler was one link, poetry a second, and tuberculosis a third, for Janet Lewis too was soon forced to go off to Sunmount, where—after nearly five years—she also recovered. Hers was a close call. The two married in 1926—Janet Lewis was still in Sunmount and Yvor Winters still teaching in Idaho, from whence he carried on an intense correspondence, largely about poetics, with Hart Crane, Allen Tate, and others. Once Janet Lewis was well, the young couple moved to California and Winters took up the professorship at Stanford that he was to hold for the rest of his life.

Together the two writers raised children (two), Airedales and goats (many), and—one might say—poets: ranks upon ranks of poets who came to learn from Winters; in their memoirs he is still legend. He wrote his books, Janet wrote hers. To his enemies in criticism—at various times they included the Agrarians (particularly John Crowe Ransom), Eliot, Pound, R. P. Blackmur, and many others—Yvor Winters was a bruiser, a kind of absolutist gladiator who struck often and with considerable accuracy at flaws in a poem or a critical system. To poets—from Hart Crane on to J.V. Cunningham, Donald Justice, Donald Hall, Thom Gunn, Ann Stanford, Robert Haas, and many others—he was a kind of Apostle, though of course they felt varying degrees of allegiance to his beliefs about poetry and of attachment to the man himself; but to Janet Lewis he was, for forty-two years, a much-treasured husband, as she makes clear in an audiotape made twenty years after his death. The cut of that grief went very deep; his name, A. Yvor Winters, is still on the mailbox of their modest house in Los Altos.

Of all the above mentioned, Wheeler and Westcott, Crane, Tate, Williams, Marianne Moore, and Yvor Winters are gone, but Janet Lewis lives on, for the most part happily, in Los Altos; her

sight has weakened but not her spirit. She has published poetry
in every decade of this century except the first, poetry that has
never lacked for champions. One of the most ardent, at present,
is Thom Gunn, who had this to say about her most recent collection, *The Dear Past* (1994):

> I think she should be getting the closest attention.
> In this collection of old age, almost incredibly, she
> is simultaneously as stringent and sweet-natured, as
> sharp and generous as she was throughout the *Col-
> lected Poems*. She is as ever deceptively simple. That
> is, hers is the best kind of simplicity, because it con-
> tains an implied complexity. . . .

The Dear Past reprints poems published between 1918 and
1991, a wingspan all but incredible, and made the more so by
the clarity and authority of a voice she has sustained for so long:
a voice that is considered, lucid, spare, and tough on itself in a
high Midwestern way. Though perhaps less imperatively than
her husband, she too has touched many poets, from the time
of Hart Crane to the time of Robert Haas. Of her verse she has
kept and reprinted only about a poem a year, taking her time
and finishing her work; luckily she has been granted a great
deal of time to take.

In addition to the poetry Janet Lewis has written two children's books, six books of prose, four libretti, and a number
of chorales. Though I am mainly concerned in this essay to
applaud and perhaps bring new readers to the three remarkable historical novels she published between 1941 and 1959, I
do think that Janet Lewis's more than eighty years of vigorous, variegated, and steady devotion to literature deserves a salute. She is a striking example of a quiet talent working quietly
through almost the entirety of a noisy, celebrity-heavy century.

From so much attention one would expect a masterpiece,
and it too is there, *The Wife of Martin Guerre* (1941), the story
of an artifice so skillful, so confusing to its victims, that simple

honesty is defeated and a good woman brought to ruin.1 It's a short novel that can run with *Billy Budd, The Spoils of Poynton, Seize the Day*, or any other of the thoroughbred novellas that might be brought to the gate.

In a statement given to Stanley Kunitz and Howard Haycraft for the 1955 edition of that still-invaluable reference work *Twentieth Century Authors*, Janet Lewis made a couple of intriguing statements. She mentions her husband's standing as a breeder of Airedales, but says nothing about his fame as a literary critic, encouraging us to suspect that the much-feared Yvor Winters, one of the hardest hitters of the bare-knucklers who slugged it out in the bloody pit of criticism as it was in the Thirties and Forties, may really have put more of his heart into his dogs. About herself she has this to say:

> I have lived a life rather lacking in "events" but with a rich and in the main very happy background. This sort of life does not provide a very interesting brief biography. The interest is chiefly in the background, which can't be treated briefly and still be interesting.

Though that statement was made forty-three years ago, I doubt she would modify it much today.

2.

That life began in Chicago, in 1899. (Janet, who is often amused, was particularly amused recently when a schoolgirl pointed out that if she makes it another couple of years she'll have lived in three centuries.) Her father, Edwin Herbert Lewis, a teacher and writer, encouraged his children's artistic leanings from the first. Her brother, Herbert Lewis, designed the dust jacket and endpapers for her first work of prose, *The Invasion* (1931). She went to the same Oak Park high school as Hemingway, at the same time, and was friends with his sister Marcelline, who was in her French club. "So I heard a lot about Ernie," she says now. She and Hemingway each have a poem in the January 1923 issue of *Poetry*.

The Lewises, like the Hemingways, had a summer place up in Michigan, in the Lewises' case way up, on an island in the St. Mary's River, midway between Mackinac and the Sault Ste. Marie. She includes three or four up-in-Michigan stories in the collection *Good-Bye, Son*, stories which contrast interestingly with Hemingway's Michigan stories. The emotional saw-teeth beneath the clear surface of Hemingway's prose are not there in Janet Lewis, though, like as not, her stories are more overtly tragic than his. In stories such as "Proserpina," "River," and "Nell," the local tragedies and misfortunes—a kindly drunk's drowning, an appealing young woman self-thwarted—are ringed with a soft Midwestern melancholy closer in tone to Sherwood Anderson or Edgar Lee Masters than to the pre-existential edginess of Hemingway. The St. Mary's River country she describes in *The Invasion* is that country unspoiled, as it was in the eighteenth and nineteenth centuries; but in his "Big Two-Hearted River" the same country is despoiled, the scarred terrain a natural metaphor for burnout. Janet Lewis had been happy in Michigan; she saw it as a fullness, whereas for Hemingway it seemed to accentuate the absences in life.

Another difference is that her interest in Michigan, once it went beyond the responses of an enraptured child on a summer outing, was historical. She made Ojibway friends, and was soon deep in the history of that much-disputed region: first Indian, then French, then British, then American, and always, after the French arrived, *métis*. *The Invasion* is an imaginative history of the founding Johnston family, a family in which Scotch-Irish and Indian blood soon mixed. It happened to be the family, too, into which the pioneering ethnographer Henry Schoolcraft married, a distant result of which was *Hiawatha*, Mr. Longfellow having depended more than a little on Henry Schoolcraft's researches. Janet Lewis has always insisted that *The Invasion* is a "narrative," not a novel; whatever one calls it, it is a confident, pungently written first book, with close attention paid to the densities, the shading, and the smells of the Northern forests and its peoples, at the time when the Americans first came to them.

That Janet Lewis, the woman, was less depressed than her schoolmate Ernest Hemingway is not to suggest that her work is Pollyanna-ish; the message of her major fiction is very dark indeed. She comes back again and again to the fate of honesty in a violent world. Her novels are tragedies, and this despite the fact that she was the product of a happy family, and, as a wife and mother, helped mold a happy family. The calm of her prose, and of the best of her verse, is a hard-won—indeed, a philosophic—calm. No one, saint or poet, could have lived through almost the entire twentieth century—or any century—and remained undisturbed. It is what she makes of her disturbances, as she struggles to keep her balance and do her duty, that is impressive. Not for nothing was the little magazine that she and her husband published for a single year in the late twenties called *The Gyroscope:* the instrument that spins and yet does not lose its balance.

Hart Crane was awed by Yvor Winters's learning—why, he could even read Portuguese!—and so impressed by his sensitivity to poetry that he allowed him to midwife *The Bridge*, rather as Pound had midwifed *The Waste Land*; and, though there was an ugly quarrel once Winters's harsh, disappointed review of the finished poem came out, Crane had not been entirely wrong to trust Winters's ear and his sensitivity. Yvor Winters from the first put the act of evaluation at the center of his critical practice. In *The Armed Vision* Stanley Edgar Hyman poked fun at some of Winters's wilder overestimations—Elizabeth Baryush, Jones Very, Sturge Moore—but he still respected Winters's force as a critic. This essay is about Janet Lewis, not Yvor Winters, but it is, I think, of interest that all Janet Lewis's major fiction hinges on the difficulty of just and accurate evaluation, not merely in the law but in the mundane circumstances of everyday life, where the consequences of misevaluation are apt to be more destructive than they usually are in literary criticism. Something of the evaluative habits of the poet-critic husband soaked deep into the creative practices of the poet-novelist wife.

The Winterses were not wealthy; professors were not then superstars. Janet Lewis wanted to write fiction for magazines that paid money, so as to add her tiny bit to the family coffers. But she was not by nature a good plotter, and was only now and then able to sell something to the slicks. Sometime in the Thirties Yvor Winters was lent an old law book, a nineteenth-century compilation of famous cases of circumstantial evidence. At some point Winters handed the book to his wife, thinking there might be something in it that would help her with her plots.

Did it ever! Though not quickly. At first she merely took notes and reflected, but the notes sprouted and in time she produced the three novels of her maturity: *The Wife of Martin Guerre* (1941), *The Trial of Sören Qvist* (1947), and *The Ghost of Monsieur Scarron* (1959). Though it is not likely that the family finances were much affected, Janet Lewis *did* learn to plot. She tells three stories in which the fate of honest people depends on their ability or inability to correctly evaluate the confusing body of evidence that life presents us as we go rushing through it. In all three cases it is the human, not the judicial, misevaluation that makes the books so powerful.

3.

Whoa, though. Despite the steady and loyal readership these three novels have won her, Janet Lewis thinks of herself mostly as a poet. Poetry is what she began with and what she still has now. She started with Imagism, the vogue of her youth, but she soon developed a less impersonal, more individual, and more complex poetic style. One would be foolish to try to guess where she'll finish up, since so far she's shown no inclination to finish at all. She has always looked closely, and with delight, at the natural world and has rendered it vividly both in verse and prose. Some of her poems have come from contemplation of her garden, or her goats, or just the morning light:

> *The path*
> *The spider makes through the air,*
> *Invisible,*
> *Until the light touches it.*
>
> *The path*
> *The light takes through the air,*
> *Invisible,*
> *Until it finds the spider's web.*

I won't attempt to follow Janet Lewis through the many decades of adding and subtracting, winnowing and honing, that have boiled down to the poems in her most recent selection, but I would like to link in a brief way one set or sequence of poems to the prime concerns of her fiction, specifically her powerful desire for balance; she doesn't want to be swept away, or altered in her nature, however violent or whatever the character of the storms that strike her. This need for balance doesn't deny sentiment—she has plenty of that—but attempts to secure for sentiment its due dignity.2

In the interview mentioned earlier, she makes clear that the death of Yvor Winters was a devastating blow; for a time after it she wrote nothing. But she did go back to the desert, to the places of the pueblo peoples, the Hopi and Navajo, peoples who appear to live in harmony with the eternal simplicities: sun, stone, sky. She ponders a fossil:

> *In quiet dark transformed to stone,*
> *Cell after cell to crystal grown,*
> *The pattern stays, the substance gone. . . .*

And, in a museum in Tucson, contemplates—at first with envy—
the mummy of a small Anasazi woman:

> *How, unconfused, she met the morning sun,*
> *And the pure sky of night,*
> *Knowing no land beyond the great horizons . . .*

But later she learns of the massacre at Awatobi (1700), where
defenders of the old gods wiped out a village that had accepted the new gods of the Spaniards; she realizes that the
little woman may not have been spared confusion and terror
after all:

> *Men of Awátobi,*
> *Killed by men of the Three Mesas,*
> *By arrow, by fire,*
> *Betrayed, trapped in their own kivas.*
>   *. . .*
> *The men of the Three Mesas,*
> *In terror for the peace of the great kachinas*
> *Who hold the world together,*
> *Who hold creation in balance,*
> *Took council, acted. . . .*

In bereavement Janet Lewis sought, even as she had in the
happy *Gyroscope* years, the secret of things that move but are
not changed:

> *The sunlight pours unshaken through the wind . . .*

And she takes a poet's delight in the fact that the Navajo, who
simplify many things, cannot reduce water to one name:

> *Tsaile, Chinle,*
> *Water flowing in, flowing out.*

Still water caught in a pool,
Caught in a gourd;
Water upon the lips, in the throat,
Falling upon long hair
Loosened in ceremony;
Fringes of rain sweeping darkly
From the dark side of a cloud,
Riding the air in sunlight,
Issuing cold from a rock,
Transparent as air, or darkened
With earth, bloodstained, grief-heavy;
In a country of no dew, snow
Softly piled, or stinging
In a bitter wind.

The earth and sun were constant,
But water,
How could they name it with one word?

In poetry Janet Lewis developed a singularity of voice over time, but in prose she was from the first strikingly confident. Here is the opening paragraph of *The Invasion*; we are on the Plains of Abraham in 1759:

> That September day the English appeared so suddenly that they seemed to have dropped from the sky; appeared, and fired. A warm rain fell now and again upon the troops, and the smoke from the rifles lay in long white streamers, dissipating slowly. The noise of the rifles, reflected from the running water and from the cliffs, was something like thunder, but the rain was too quiet. And running, for the French, had become almost more important than fighting. The head

of Montcalm lay upon the breast of Ma-mongazid, the young Ojibway, the dark sorrowful face, with its war paint of vermilion and white, intent above the French face graying rapidly. Presently they took the Marquis to the hospital in St. Charles, where he died. Ma-mongazid with his warriors in thirty bark canoes returned to La Pointe Chegoimegon through the yellowing woods and the increasing storms of autumn. The rule of the French was over, the Province of Michilimackinac had become the Northwest Territory. The Ojibways called the English Saugaunosh, the Dropped-from-the-Clouds, and regretted the French.

With similar confidence she brings us to Jutland in the early seventeenth century, as she opens the story of the parson of Vejlby, Sören Qvist:

> The inn lay in a hollow, the low hill, wooded with leafless beech trees, rising behind it in a gentle round just high enough to break the good draft from the inn chimneys, so that on this chill day the smoke rose a little and then fell downward. The air was clouded with dampness. It was late November, late in the afternoon, but no sunlight came from the west, and to the east the sky was walled with cloud where the cold fog thickened above the shores of Jutland. There was the smell of sea in the air even these few miles inland, but the foot traveler who had come upon sight of the inn had been so close to the sea for so many days now that he was unaware of the salty fragrance. . . .

and to Gascony almost a century earlier, as she begins *Martin Guerre*:

> One morning in January, 1539, a wedding was celebrated in the village of Artigues. That night the two children who had been espoused to one another lay in

bed in the house of the groom's father. They were Bertrande de Rols, aged eleven years, and Martin Guerre, who was no older, both offspring of rich peasant families as ancient, as feudal and as proud as any of the great seignorial houses of Gascony. The room was cold. Outside the snow lay thinly over the stony ground, or, gathered into long shallow drifts at the corners of houses, left the earth bare. But higher, it extended upward in great sheets and dunes, mantling the ridges and choking the wooded valleys, toward the peak of La Bacanère and the long ridge of Le Burat, and to the south, beyond the long valley of Luchon, the granite Maladetta stood sheathed in ice and snow. . . .

The movement backward, into earlier centuries, which might inhibit many writers, seems to excite Janet Lewis and also to increase her assurance. When she comes into her own time, as she does in her one conventional novel of manners, *Against a Darkening Sky* (1943), set in Santa Clara County during the Depression, she is noticeably less confident. The heroine of that book is introduced to us as Mary Perrault, but is often thereafter called Mrs. Perrault, as if the author is not sure just how much intimacy she should assume with her main character.

In a way the three historical novels, all based on actual cases in the law, are legal briefs brought to life, the novelist being a prosecutor whose sympathies are nonetheless with the accused; and the accused, in all cases, become the condemned. There is nothing quite like these three books in our fiction; such echoes as there are are French, particularly Stendhal. All the central characters, whether Bertrande de Rols, or Pastor Sören, or the honest bookbinder Jean Larcher, are threatened by judicial confusion over circumstantial evidence, but the brilliance of the pattern is the way in which Janet Lewis shows that none of the three would ever have been in court in the first place had they themselves not made similar misjudgments when confronted with the rushing mass of circumstantial evidence in everyday life.

Perhaps the best example of such normal error occurs in *The Ghost of Monsieur Scarron*. Paul Damas, the apprentice bookbinder who has seduced his master's wife, Marianne, loses a button from his shirt:

> One day in midsummer, Paul and Marianne being alone in the bindery, Paul remarked that he had lost a button from his shirt, and Marianne offered to sew it on for him.
>
> It seemed an innocent activity, especially in view of their relationship. She performed the task deftly and quickly, then looked about for her scissors to snip the thread. Not finding them, "Lend me your knife," she said to Paul. "No, never mind," and, bending toward him, she bit the thread. The action brought her head against his breast. Perhaps she held it there the fraction of a moment longer than was necessary. It seemed to Paul that she delayed the moment, for, looking over her head, he met the surprised gaze of his master. Jean had returned, with no undue quietness of step, with no intention of taking anyone unawares, but absorbed in themselves, neither Paul nor Marianne had heard the opening of the door or the advancing step. A rigidity in Paul warned Marianne of something amiss. She lifted her head, looked first at Paul, then followed his glance toward her husband.
>
> Midday, midsummer, the air was warm and moist after a morning shower. Marianne had discarded her cap and her fichu. Her arms were bare almost to the shoulder, as she had pushed back her sleeves. The air,

the informality of the moment, the two figures standing like one in a rectangle of sunlight, all combined to give Jean an impression of what was in fact the truth. But the moment itself was innocent.

A sense of revelation rushed upon him, bringing to mind a hundred hitherto unquestioned gestures, poses, inflections. They were lovers, these two. He had taken his wife in adultery. . . . He stopped dead where he stood. Then the moment resolved itself naturally, without drama. Marianne came toward him, holding on the middle finger of the hand poised above her, her silver thimble. . . .

"I mislaid my scissors," she said. "I had to use my teeth." . . .

Jean's fear and knowledge turned about him and then leveled into an illusion. Nothing was wrong. . . .

There you have the pregnant, and, in this case, fatal, error. Jean Larcher had read the action correctly, had seen the avidity in his wife's face and in her bite; and yet he talks himself out of it. Had he held to his true perception and thrown his adulterous wife and treacherous apprentice out at this juncture, he would have saved himself torture and death. But he suborned his own sound judgment, in this case tragically.

The human tendency to dissuade oneself from accurate insight surfaces rather more complexly in the story of Sören Qvist, a good pastor at war with himself because of his uncontrollable angers. Pastor Sören has a real enemy, one Morten Bruus, who tricks him, but it is really the force of the Pastor's faith-driven self-accusation that causes the trick to work: he convinces himself that he has killed Morten Bruus's brother, though the brother, in fact, is not dead.

Reading the three novels in a line, from *The Wife of Martin Guerre* to *The Ghost of Monsieur Scarron*, is a powerful experience. Though all three were based on actual cases in the law, their power is literary not legal. In each story a son leaves home because of strife with the father, and returns too late to save the family. In each the ruin of an honest person is complete, and in each there is a fully and vividly realized woman who finds herself twisting helplessly in the dilemmas posed by love and duty. To each of these women—Bertrande de Rols, Anna Sörensdaughter, and Marianne Larcher—Janet Lewis might say what she says to the mummy of the Anasazi woman in Tucson, "my sister, my friend," for she knows these women: their feelings, their gestures, their happiness, their changeability, and their stunned helplessness as they see doom approaching.

Anna Sörensdaughter has her happiness destroyed when the young judge she loves and is engaged to marry has to pass the sentence of death on her father. Bertrande de Rols must finally accuse the nice imposter who is kind to her because she can but for so long live a lie; she chooses truth over love and then is dismissed with perfect coldness when the real Martin Guerre comes back and discovers that she has dishonored him. Marianne Larcher is the weakest of the three women, so physically in thrall to the young apprentice that she will do anything for him; but she is no less appealing for being blindly dependent, even though it results in her good husband being condemned. The last words of the Martin Guerre story might serve as ending for all these novels:

> Of Martin Guerre nothing more is recorded, whether he returned to the wars or remained in Artigues, nor is there further record of Bertrande de Rols, his wife. But when hate and love have together exhausted the soul, the body seldom endures for long.

In the old law book her husband lent her, Janet Lewis discerned a great theme: the limitations of human judgment, not merely between judge and accused but between husband and wife, father and son, king and counselor (for it was a little burlesque in the manner of the late Monsieur Scarron, insulting Madame de Maintenon, that resulted in the execution of the honest bookbinder). She discerned it and, for a span of some twenty years in her long life, had the intelligence, the persistence, and the force to be equal to it.

Auden reminded us definitively that it's language Time worships: not wisdom or innocence or physical beauty or, I would add, length of life. Janet Lewis has indeed lived a long time, but what is important is that all through that long time she has continued to tell the stories that have meant something to her in a manner all her own, and with a distinction of language that will carry them forward to startle and delight readers yet to come.

4.

Though I was at Stanford in 1960 I failed to meet Janet Lewis. Now and then I would see her husband proceeding in Johnsonian fashion through the college, often with a Boswell or two tugging at his sleeves, but, at the time, it was *her* work that excited me, an excitement that came back with its old force when I reread her recently.

So I ventured a letter and, to my delight, she promptly called me in Texas and invited me to dinner on Valentine's Day of this year. She didn't sound like the grandmother of fiction, either, when she called; she just sounded like a well-spoken woman who was curious about what a writer from Texas would make of her work.

I arrived at her home in Los Altos hand in hand with El Niño; the abundant vegetation that must once have enticed her goats dripped from every leaf and stem. I felt like the person who was going to meet the person who had once seen Shelley plain—Shelley in this case being Hart Crane, who had visited the Winterses at Christmas in 1927. Janet, still convalescent, gave him tea in her bedroom, which, at the time, she was rarely allowed to leave. "Oh yes," she said, when I mentioned that tea. "He was very polite." Despite the breach that occurred over her husband's review of *The Bridge*, the Winterses were both deeply grieved when Hart Crane killed himself by jumping off the boat.

Janet too is very polite, but she's neither fussy nor chilly. She's lived in that smallish but cheerful house for sixty-four years and is thoroughly the mistress of it; there she raised her family, there she watched war come and war be over, there she entertained generations of poets, artists, musicians, and even the occasional lepidopterist such as Vladimir Nabokov, who showed up at her door with his butterfly net one day in 1941. The Nabokovs and the Winterses hit it off; the exiles came often for meals. I had heard that Nabokov enjoyed himself so much in her kitchen that he sometimes helped her wash up; when I asked her about this she chuckled and said, "Why, I wouldn't be surprised if he had."

I had hardly said hello when we were off through the streaming backyard to the small, detached study where she and Yvor Winters did their writing; an old Royal typewriter sits as a reminder of those days. On the walls, casually tacked up, were photographs of a number of noble Airedales and several slightly less noble poets, one or two of them so obscure that neither of us could quite puzzle out who they might be. A sketch of Pound was by one window; a lovely photograph of Janet as a young woman hung from a nail. Janet remarked that the goats came into her life at a time when she was too weak to write but liked to sketch; Yvor Winters went down the road and bought a couple of goats, so his wife could have something to sketch besides Airedales.

Later, two gifted men friends turned up and cooked a delicious meal, which we ate at the small table in her kitchen. Once, on the audiotape, when a young interviewer was asking her how she got the details right in her historical fiction, Janet talked for a bit about looking at Breughel and reading lots of histories, but then she dropped from the highfalutin' and merely said, "I've always liked kitchens"; it is as if she is saying that from her own bright kitchen, where Vladimir Nabokov once wielded a dish towel, she can imagine all kitchens, as her fiction—filled with kitchens—demonstrates.

In the company of most people who are brushing a century, ignoring their age requires conscious effort; but when Janet Lewis is discussing a book or remembering a visit or a trip, or describing northern Michigan as it was in her girlhood, *remembering* that she's elderly is what takes the conscious effort. Perhaps the fact that her sickness was so nearly mortal, that she lived for five years of her young womanhood with death as a near-neighbor, has left her unimpressed that it's in the neighborhood still. Though she is reasonably cautious, and is attended by squadrons of friends, who do their attending for the rich reward of her company, there is also a slightly mischievous, slightly devil-may-care, I'll-go-when-I'm-good-and-ready air about her. It's as if that terribly early struggle has bought her a little exemption, and she knows it, and she means to enjoy her privileges to the full.

The four of us finished the meal very companionably, had dessert, had more tea. Janet probed around in a bookcase and found an essay on her poetry that she thought I might like to read. I took it and wandered back to my motel on the Camino, thrilled. A great lady of American letters had—for the space of an evening—been my valentine.

Notes

1. For a skillful unraveling of the complex history behind the Martin Guerre story, readers are referred to *The Return of Martin Guerre*, by Natalie Zemon Davis (Harvard University Press, 1983).

2. *Landscape, Memory, and the Poetry of Janet Lewis*, by Brigitte Carnochan, an excellent short study, was published by the Stanford Libraries and English Department in 1995.